Montezuma's
Treasure Canyon

ED GILBERT

THE STORY

The major character in the story is Troy O'Neill, an Arizona boy reared by a religious mother of Dutch heritage and an adventurous Irish father. The boy treks northward into the wilds of the mountains and canyons of Utah in search of an ancient Aztec treasure.

Amid harrowing experiences and life or death struggles, the impossible dream comes true.

INTRODUCTION

Although a work of fiction. "Montezuma's Treasure Canyon" is based upon legends and accounts of places and people as they once did or do exist. From my prospecting sojourns and adventures, as well as studies of old records and writings, I believe that a fabulous treasure—much as that described herein—could actually exist. Perhaps it is somewhere near the area described within this writing, and perhaps it is not.

At this point, I wish to caution would-be treasure seekers that this is indeed a work of fiction, and, although there are actual and similar names of places that exist, there is no known evidence of any such find within such boundaries. Therefore, I discourage any and all unauthorized invasions into the areas that are obviously described. Indeed, much of said territory is private property or otherwise state or federally owned . . . I authorize no publisher to print any of this material in any form less the inclusion of this disclaimer or one of similar intent.

ACKNOWLEDGEMENTS

I wish to acknowledge the following, which have contributed to some of the descriptive materials herein: the Utah Travel Council of Salt Lake City, The National Geographic Society, the State Road Commission of Utah, and The Library of Congress.

A special thanks must go to my friends, Gerry Vandlen and Gary Manley. Without their assistance this book could not have been published.

Thanks also to Sara Manley, a student at Kendall College of Art and Design, who painted the cover page art using a watercolor format and Nancy Hart, Watercolor Illustration Professor, who advised her.

And of course I give utmost thanks to a neighbor and friend, Ruth Lantinga, who accomplished the original stylized artwork within this book.

Last, but of highest importance, I wish to thank my son, Steven, who recently received a degree in anthropology—for it was his young persistence in dragging this unworthy person on many an adventure over and through the far-flung mountains and deserts of the Southwest that spawned the idea for this story.

PROLOGUE

Sixty million years ago, ancient streams cascaded and twisted their way toward a large inland lake within an area one day to become known as southern Utah. Suddenly, the earth heaved mightily, and the strata of sediment and sand was catapulted nearly two miles above sea level. Gradually, the formation hardened, and several million years later the huge mass started to crack, while along its many fissures and traces ice and water began a timed artistry.

Huge sculptures and monoliths tinted with oxides of manganese and iron began slowly to emerge, some in a pink or vivid and flaming red, others in an eggshell, almost transparent white. The large plateau, once thrust over nine thousand feet skyward, was slowly becoming shattered into a bewitching amphitheater that took on the appearance of a ghost-like city of winding alleys and Javanese spires . . . as though God had built a fairyland of chessmen and temples out of solid rock and stood aside to cast a spell of enchantment over the huge buttresses.

Over more millions of years, nature carried out the plan, as she continued to gnash her teeth and etch her work. And, as the earth trembled along and near the Paunsaugunt Fault, she concluded her architecture of the canyon.

Perhaps not unwittingly, she had prepared it for the age of mammals—already paralleling and in many ways more than equaling the enchantment that existed here. Perhaps too, she had prepared it for the mysterious secret that it would one day have hidden within its bowels.

The year was 1520 . . . It was a stifling evening in late June, and from this seven-thousand-foot promontory, equidistant of the towering structures, the Pyramid of The Sun and the pyramid of The Moon, one could not only see but feel the powers of the Great Gulf mirrored to the east and the frothed, green expanses of the Wide Waters stretching westward.

Montezuma, Emperor of the Aztec nation, was the one positioned at this singularly important apex, which towered over the lush islands and pristine lakes.

The statuesque figure of forty years removed his plumed and jeweled crown of gold and placed it reverently aside upon his cotton mantle. Then he stood naked, except for his waistband and ornamented breech clout, sinewy arms poised overhead and fingers curled into the sulfurous air—as though reaching to gather strength from the heat-shimmering moon and the bright, elusive stars.

Montezuma spoke sternly to his gods, with voice smacking interrogation and impatience, and his black, stone-like eyes searching the heavens.

"Hear me! This Valley of Mexico has been the home of my people for two thousand years . . . You, the Gods of Teotihuacan of the ages past, are still our Gods: For you we have fertilized these lands, offered sacrifice, and prospered with the wealth of many generations . . . We are a mighty and dominant nation.

"Under my father, Ilhuicamina, the great warrior and law giver, we have constructed many temples and pyramids to Tenochtitlan. We have waged successful warfare to the Great Gulf itself.

MONTEZUMA SPOKE STERNLY
TO HIS GODS, WITH VOICE
SMACKING OF INTERROGATION
AND IMPATIENCE.

"For years," his chiseled lips vibrated through the blanketed sky, as he turned, arching his back toward the moon, "I have believed my father's prophecy that the great white god, Quetzalcoatl, would one day rise from the eastern waters to again rule all of Mexico . . . Now it seems that the emissary of this god, the Spaniard who is called Hernan Cortez by his armor-clad warriors, has returned."

Montezuma turned his clay-smooth face over his shoulder toward the moon and then swiveled to clench a hairy fist at it. He exclaimed enigmatically, "Why then, do I now feel this despair within my heart? I know it is the despair of coming disaster for my people!

"I have presented this god's strange general with riches far beyond mere gifts. He but gloats and waits for more . . . No! Rather he lusts for it like a pig! My people fear him and his mighty warriors, and now I confess that I too fear—fear that my life will be taken before I can save my people. The time is urgent! At this very moment, many of our own warriors meet to discuss the choosing of a new, younger and stronger leader . . . I ask you, the mighty gods, for an answer now!"

The silence after his verbal onslaught was loud and ominous, but his gods remained taciturn while his ears were deafened with the ring of his own voice. Montezuma lowered his tear-stained cheeks to a level and looked out over his city of three hundred thousand people. His hands fell dejectedly to his sides and he turned slowly toward his guards. Then a downward glance brought the mighty warrior to a startled and swift halt. He stood transfixed in thought as he watched the moonbeams play back at his eyes from a thousand twinkling facets in his jewel-encrusted crown. Then a smile slowly washed over his face as he stooped, picked it up, and looked it over thoughtfully.

It was an overcast, subdued twilight of the following morning that found Montezuma standing before the hastily assembled caravan. His amber eyes flicked over each of the 50 laden burros and in turn to each of the 18 warriors in silver armor.

Now the emperor quickly motioned two of his most trusted officers aside, one of whom was his own nephew. He led them to a remote position alongside the protective aqueduct. Peering at lengths to be certain other eyes were not witnesses, he knelt and sketched a crude map in the sand. He drew with a forefinger, carefully indicating the Great Gulf to the east, the Giant Waters westward, and a large land mass to the north. In the latter, he sketched a large mountain range and indicated a nearby, sizable river. Then he broke a Cacao stick, removed its blossoms with a show of respect, and jabbed it deep into the sand near an intersecting point but slightly to the north of the river.

"Here," Montezuma said simply but definitely, "Here is where you are to go. In your long journey you will find deserts with sand hot as fire, and larger than the Great Gulf; you will cross a void as deep as the bowels of the earth.

"At this place you will find our original people, the Uto-Aztecans, who held that land thousands of years before they wandered to this place to become your very ancestors . . . But they are still your brothers and perhaps can be trusted." He paused thoughtfully, then said conclusively, "And perhaps they cannot. It will be best to place trust in no one, if that is possible."

Montezuma looked each officer directly in the eyes with deep admiration. Then, as he brushed away traces of the map, he spoke softly to them for a final time. "You have in your trust, much of the treasure of our people—gathered over more than sixty generations. No one must know, and it is of extreme importance that no one remains alive to tell." He hesitated and looked slowly one to the other. "Do you know exactly what it is I say?"

The grim-lipped emissaries nodded, the only acknowledgement that was necessary.

And so it was that the last great Aztec leader symbolically stood atop the aqueduct that his father had designed and created, to watch the significant heavily laden caravan wind its way among the moats to disappear to the northwest. Montezuma thought of the jeweled gold and silver treasures for a long moment, then lifted arms, eyes and voice to his gods. This time, however, it was a quiet and thankful offering.

But Montezuma's thanks was to be short-lived, for on that very day he was taken hostage by Cortez.

On June 25th of the year 1520, the Emperor found himself facing impossible odds from disposed followers and enemy alike, and fell victim to stones hurled by his own subjects as he attempted to calm them against threats proclaimed by the invading Cortez.

It was the "Sorrowful Night" of June 30th, and the Aztec empire had fallen. Yet, as Montezuma lay painfully in his final moments, wounded in head, arm and leg, a smile came to play upon his lips . . . He knew not where his soul would rest—if ever—but he was assured that the Montezuma trail would remain. At this moment, it was winding its way safely to the north.

CHAPTER 1

THE YEAR WAS 1875 . . . The rider suddenly reined up, a whistle of wonderment frozen on his lips as he carefully approached the great chasm. The unexpected jerk on the bit sent his wiry, Mescalero-bred mustang into a dangerous side-step, so the young, lean rider slipped from the saddle and held the fire-eyed sorrel. Again he gazed down and across the deep crimson rent.

Troy O'Neill had seen many and varied landscapes, but never one that compared to this. His bright and intelligent blue eyes scanned the beautiful while frightening spectacle. Yellow limestone framed the canyon rim in either direction, while as far as the eye could see, precipitous cliffs fell into purple, seemingly bottomless depths.

The young rider knew from history that this could be none other than the awesome abyss known as the Grand Canyon del Rio Colorado: so named by the Spanish explorer, Coronado, the first white man to claim its sighting, back in 1540. It encompassed over a thousand square miles, and a mighty river, the Colorado, flowed wildly through its depths, making it the world's showplace of erosion.

Although transfixed and awed on the moment, he felt an over-whelming weariness throughout his body. It had been a long and devastating trail up from Payson, in the Arizona-New Mexican Territory. He'd weathered the cliffs of the Mogollon (Muggy-own) Rim, immense lightning storms through the tall pines of the Coconino, and then the desert heat of Flag. Piled on this had been more days of stifling dust and furnace winds through the Painted Desert. The young cowboy was bone-weary.

Troy O'Neill ground-reined Sundown and stumbled about preparing a makeshift camp. He partook of a brief but hearty meal of warmed-over beef jerky and biscuits, gazing long into the embers of a small fire. Finally, he exhaled deeply and relaxed, viewing the sunset that seemed to cataract along the canyon's distant rim. Suddenly he was overcome with a burst of inner spirit . . . He was heading toward what may be the most fabulous of adventures, into the wild Utah Territory. And, he was young and thirsting for adventure and excitement.

Shortly after his twentieth birthday, he had made his decision to make this venture, and now he recalled how hard it had been—hearing his father's words and parting shots of wisdom as he prepared to leave their Arizona ranch . . . He had held some misgiving about leaving his father, alone with Troy since his mother had died nearly a year earlier. But in the end he had gone, and he felt certain his mother would have wanted him to follow such a quest.

Kate O'Neill had been born of sturdy stock. Her father had immigrated to the Pennsylvania coal fields from Ireland in 1820, where he had wed Caroline VanDuin, the daughter of Dutch immigrants.

Kate's early years were spent within a highly religious atmosphere, her mother being a devout subject of the German Reformed Church, which had been renamed The Reformed Church in the United States in 1869.

Along with her devout religious feelings, however, Kate had harbored a deep wanderlust for excitement and adventure. Thus she had married a young, personable man named George O'Neill, who was determined to seek a fortune in the gold fields of the Arizona-New Mexico Territory.

Kate O'Neill was not by nature a frail woman; however, circumstances proved her undoing. She had recently and literally worked life and limb away at the small ranch in Payson while her husband and her brother-in-law, Jim O'Neill, had been off with many others of their Irish clan constructing the Union Pacific Railway.

But Kate was perhaps stronger in another way, and for many years had spent long hours teaching a love for reading and writing to Troy.

Troy's mother had likewise been selective in her son's reading material. Much time had been devoted to study of the Bible, which Troy read daily and still carried faithfully in his saddlebag at all times.

However, in the more recent years, Troy had also developed a root-liking for the field of archaeology, several books on which his mother had arranged to have forwarded west from a New York university.

While never forcing her feelings upon her son, Kate's obvious aim for Troy was toward joining the ministry. She offered no complaint concerning his archaeological pursuits, beyond instilling the thought that he might strive to find a positive relationship between it and the Bible. And, although many theories found in his archaeology books differed sharply with biblical readings, Troy was determined to study both, reasoning also that were his mother alive she would not be against his present quest.

The youngster had also been an apt listener, and had done so many an hour as both father and uncle related harrowing tales concerning the construction of the mighty U.P. Railroad through and beyond the savage wilderness . . . How they, the Irish clan, had frequently visited the gambling dens within the hastily constructed towns along the trail; how they had sweated and toiled tie by tie and rail to rail across the yellow prairies; how they had fought side by side and sometimes back to back against wolves and stampeding herds of buffalo, and how they had battled and beaten the Black Hills to move onward into the Rockies, where the fight had sifted to one of savage Indians and great, unmerciful mountains. And many times they had told with pride how they finally had stood at Promontory, Utah, upon that May day in 1869 to witness the world-famous driving of the golden spike that connected east to west.

Those had proved to be prosperous as well as adventure-filled years for John and Jim O'Neill, and the brothers had returned not only in a spirited mood but also financially rewarded. This time they also decided to abandon their earlier pastime of gold prospecting — which the non-incorporated area of Payson was noted for — and opted to get serious about horse ranching. This they did, and in an industrious and businesslike fashion. So much so that this too proved rewarding to the adventuring duo.

It was close upon their return that Troy's mother had started to show the cost of her hard existence in that yet-uncivilized mining area, and not long thereafter that she succumbed to it. The adventurers had returned with more than a little, but all of it too late for her.

Several years later the gold fever claimed Jim O'Neill once more, and he had packed northward on another prospecting venture, leaving Troy and his father to tend the expanding ranch. Uncle Jim . . . Troy kicked out, spurring another log into the fire. He thought often of that individual and imagined with no little pride that he himself had indeed inherited his uncle's spirit and fever for adventure.

Since early childhood Troy had insatiably devoured his uncle's tale, which, in addition to the railroad days plus a brief stint in the Civil War, ranged from his pony express rides from Crittenden to Point Lookout, Utah, in 1860, to the finding and losing of several fortunes in gold and silver . . . In particular there was an often repeated story of a journey into the mountainous regions of southwestern Utah, where a fabulous treasure most certainly existed—awaiting someone with the knowledge and the courage to locate it, and to bring it out.

The young rider's hand moved automatically to his shirt pocket, from which he removed and unfolded a flimsy, yellowed piece of paper. Once again, perhaps for the thousandth time, Troy O'Neill was drawn onward and into that fantastic accounting.

Jim O'Neill's lust for prospecting had indeed, but quite unwittingly, carried through a strange, harrowing experience in the wild and untamed area northeast of Kanab, Utah, in 1854.

The prospector had noted points of prominence, and in fact sketched a crude map of this strange trail, which led easterly from Kanab to a Ranchero Johnson, then along some great block peaks and pink, towering cliffs to the north. At that position he had traced a dried wash into an extinct volcanic area, and many miles thereafter the path had led upon a gigantic canyon of domes, spires, and brilliantly colored buttresses of white, red and pink. His lecturings and scrawled descriptions of the place were so vivid that Troy could envision it in his mind's eye—it had to appear as though a fantastic outdoor arena, and filled with rock sculptures, sandstone monoliths and pinnacles.

His uncle had proclaimed that the giant arena would take three days of the hardest riding to skirt end to end, and that it seemed all but impossible to enter from the southern trail, while it was actually impenetrable from many points along its rim.

The map and its notes contained little if any information or reference to the Indians in the area; however, his story related that it was upon approaching the canyon he had sighted several red natives. These savages—he had assumed they were that—had seemed more shy than hostile, and although a'foot they had very rapidly and mysteriously disappeared.

While following the light trace of these Indians, more from curiosity than for any other purpose, he had been led to a spot along the canyon's western wall where an almost undetectable, small creek wound a path downward through a narrow gorge. He had followed this rent to nearly a half mile in depth, to where three escarpments ran together in triangular fashion. There was no further sign of the natives. But here, while pondering direction, he had noticed a triangular bird-like design, carved above one of the ledges in a flat stone. The figure had been nearly obscured by scarce, climbing vegetation, but there it was, an odd-shaped petroglyph, seemingly in flight and pointing downward to the left fork.

He had thus descended another precipitous trace, and near what at first appeared a dead end had ferreted out a secretive, narrow passageway. This dark, subterranean pass had gradually widened into a cave, the mouth of which suddenly gaped outward and over the canyon floor itself.

Jim O'Neill had become excited at his find, and he gloried in expectation, thrilled that he must be privy to a discovery far beyond any of his previous encounters.

The walls of the cave had literally been covered with etchings and designs. Many were of the same, triangular bird sign. Others were of goats and various four-legged animals, while some were man-like in appearance.

Jim O'Neill's excitement was such that he hadn't noticed the approach of a stealthy figure—one suddenly standing right alongside him.

As oft as the tale had been repeated, at this point Troy's hair had always taken a perpendicular stance from his neck. But it was a short-lived feeling, as the hastened explanation always came that the intruder proved to be another prospector who had, as was the trend of the era, followed one of his peers in the hope of sharing a bonanza.

The second man was a wandering prospector named Grace. With little consultation the two men had fallen together in the adventure—this from the protective feeling of numbers rather than either man's need of the other's companionship.

Thus the pair had proceeded to explore holes and depths of the canyon and its perpendicular structures, and several weeks passed with no further compensation than the location of two similar caves and the finding of bits and pieces of pottery and bones. Then one day, while dangerously near the last of their provisions, Grace had returned to the cave, excited, out of breath and babbling with a renewed enthusiasm. In his hand he proudly brandished what appeared to be a broken or severed link of gold bracelet. It was studded with sparkling emeralds, and a few empty settings and deep scratches seemed to attest not only to its authenticity but point to its former owner's use, or perhaps abuse.

The adventurers hurried to further inspect the area of the find. And, as night closed in, near the discovery of yet another bird-like petroglyph, they found what was most certainly a carefully disguised trail which angled steeply up the wall of the canyon. With this knowledge the two had returned to their cave, gleeful with the expectation of what tomorrow would surely bring.

There was no tomorrow for Grace. Jim O'Neill awoke to find absolutely no trace of the other prospector, and a frantic but extensive search had led him to conclude that his short-term partner must have wandered out into the darkness of night and fallen to his reward from one of the many cliffs that confronted the mouth of their cave.

With renewed and dogged determination, O'Neill again located the trace along the wall and began climbing. In most areas there had been little more than tiny hand or foot holes chipped into the solid rock and sandstone, and he told how he had teetered dangerously on several occasions, fearing to cast the slightest glance downward into the jagged abyss below.

Troy shivered again as he recalled the closing moments of his uncle's account . . . Rounding a golden hued spire, which had somewhat resembled a huge queen-like figure in a dress, he stood upright to find that he was upon a large, flat shelf. This shelf was about the size of a small ranch house, and hewn flat as a table from the solid stone. Along its canyon side rose yet another, perfectly vertical and flat area of multi-coloured rock, its lower section fashioned somewhat in the shape of an arch. Within this arched area appeared a smaller, man-made, sealed entrance into the canyon wall itself.

Near the center of the smaller arch the rocks had been so arranged as to leave a series of triangular nooks. Within these shelves, untouched but powdered by the years,

IT CONTAINED A BLOODY
HEAD FROM WHICH PROTRUDED
THE HUGE EYES AND GRIZZLED
BEARD OF GRACE!

O'Neill had counted the remains of seventeen human skulls. Then his growing cautiousness and fear had intensified to the breaking point as he discovered a newly carved shelf. Placed several feet to the side of the others, it contained not another skull, but a bloody head from which protruded the huge eyes and grizzled beard of Grace!

Jim O'Neill had often explained his panicked, almost suicidal escape from that canyon; how, for three days and nights he had plunged headlong from that area, always with the feeling of someone or something immediately behind—a hot breath always upon his neck, and his beard always turned over his shoulder. The sound of footfalls had been always and immediately in his own . . .

Many years had come and gone, and a young man now folded the fragile map and returned it ceremoniously to his shirt-pocket. His eyes bore into the embers of his campfire, but his mind was far removed, and his face glowed with a fire and thirst all its own—an insatiable thirst for adventure. Troy O'Neill smiled . . . Tomorrow he would renew his journey to Kanab, where he could procure the necessary supplies.

VIRGINIA

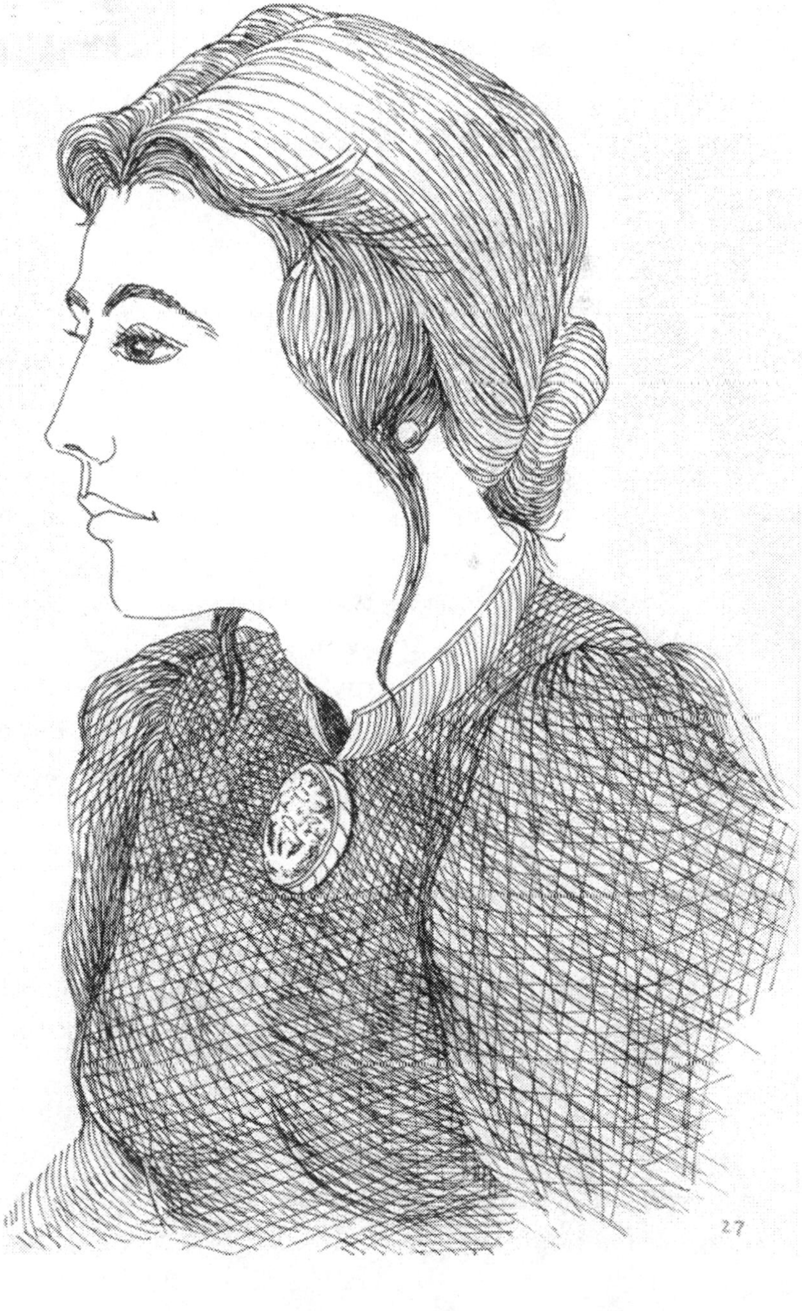

CHAPTER 2

VIRGINIA GRAYSON had become accustomed to being an attention-getter, and this time she could hardly escape the turn of the blond head and intense stare of this blue-eyed cowboy. She moved briskly onward but returned the compliment long enough to take in the lean, flat figure of the Levi-clad youngster standing alongside the red mustang. His clothes were worn and whitened considerably by alkali, and a trace of stubble sallowed his cheeks, but he seemed strangely and roughly handsome. Her eyes touched briefly upon the six-gun strapped low on the young stranger's hip, and she caught a glimpse of the large, unsharpened rowels in his ornamented spurs.

Virginia guiltily averted her eyes, and heard a low, murmuring, "Evenin' ma'am," as she did. Then she turned under the sign indicating Kanab's only dry goods store, which had been appropriately christened, SECOND TO NONE.

She boldly ventured one more glance through the window pane as she made for the counter. Here her young friend, Corabell Smithers, snapped her to reality.

"Well, if it ain't Ginny . . . Where you been hiding?"

"You know exactly where, Bell—trapped with my old magazines and books at the ranchero." Then, indicating minor interest by a raised eyebrow toward the window, she queried simply, "Who's that?"

"Just some cowpuncher who followed the up stage in 'bout half an hour ago. Been standin' out yonder ever since, pearin' around like a lost puppy . . . Why, interested?" Bell smiled slyly.

"Who wouldn't be?" Virginia flashed, with an honest indication and chin-up look at her old school chum. Then she added with rapid resignation, "Oh well, riders the looks of him just come and go. No sense in getting excited 'cause you never see them again anyway." She ran deft fingers over a bolt of green cloth that suddenly captured her interest, continuing factually, "Besides, daddy and Judd never let me out of sight far enough to meet a boy my own age. Only ones show up in Johnson are a few old prospectors and an occasional down on his luck trail rider—both looking for hand-outs!"

Bell concurred in a monotone, and her voice hummed on while Virginia became taciturn and thoughtful. She reflected upon her situation at length as she turned the bolt of hunter green over and over . . .

The town of Kanab was the closest hamlet of any size to the Grayson ranch. While not the largest boomtown of its era, it had become a crossroad of activity during the autumn of the 1800s. Miners and hopeful prospectors, alongside cattlemen and cowboys, cross to the north and south through its dusty streets. A hub in the west's great basin, its location had sprung from one of the driest regions in North America. Alkali deserts, sagebrush plains and barren mountain ranges predominated in every direction. The terrain had made for a poor existence indeed for its earlier settlers, its only real plus being that of the year-long grazing, an asset that had made a few of the area ranchers moderately successful.

Scattered bands of Indians had inhabited the entire area long before white people arrived upon the scene, and most of those sapped the better part of their energy and time digging roots and trapping small animals for food, almost existing on the edge of starvation. These Indians had remained quite docile and nonaggressive until white men began to poke about or seriously settle the territory. Most spoke the Uto-Aztecan dialect. The largest of these tribes was the Southern Paiute, and several small bands of these had become more warlike since Virginia's grandfather, Ira Johnson, had staked out a small range east of Kanab. That had taken place at the turn of the century, and gradually, as the whites tended to remain in the southern end of the canyon that marked three borders of the ranchero, the Paiute had turned to a state of semi-indifference. In such fashion, the Johnson homestead had eventually become somewhat of a small settlement, named after its first pioneer, Virginia's grandfather on her mother's side.

The elder Johnsons were hardy folk, and the type that seemed to thrive on hard work while being happy to gain a little substance from year to year. Thus in the years that passed they had eventually expanded their domain from wall to wall within the white-walled canyon they called home.

Virginia's was another story . . . This same canyon seemed of late to be no more promising than huge, unscalable prison walls. Indeed, she spent much of her time now in sulking, sorrowful moods of self-pity . . . After all, she was an attractive and adventure-seeking girl of 18—had recently discovered herself to be belle-of-the-ball at some of the infrequent dances she was allowed to attend. All this only to return from such Cinderella events or like trips into Kanab to the dreariness of the same ranch, same jeans and boots, and her horses.

John Grayson had always carried an uncommon love toward horses, and it seemed the animals had always reciprocated. He had originally formed his caballada, or remuda as he chose to call it, from Spanish mustang stock. Some of these, however, had eventually become crossed with Percheron and Morgan, along with an occasional paint, calico, or even pinto mix, which were favorite of the nearby Paiute.

As the years progressed, so had Grayson's herd. For ranch purposes, the Indian horses proved too small to handle cattle and other horses within this mountainous, canyon region, while the larger breeds could do all and more than was required of them. These were the mustangs, and they had become Virginia's favorites as well. At the young age of 12, her father allowed her a string of seven for her own use and care.

The young lady of Ranchero Johnson was an excellent rider, and became familiar with the terrain within a day's ride in all directions—the exception being northward to the canyon's interior. That area her father had implacably declared off limit to her. Lo these years it had remained Indian Territory, and the behavior of the estranged band that yet inhabited it still caused the Graysons much concern.

Thus Virginia had at first remained content to ride the trail toward Kanab, and to the south-east among the Vermillion Cliffs to the Paria Canyon area. But in recent months such trail rides had become less frequent, now almost never. She pined for other adventure.

And then came her worst complication. Her father had considered himself somewhat beholden to a hand named Judd Hazelud, a strange gunslinger who had taken her father's cause in a recent land dispute, and Grayson had subsequently named Hazelud foreman of the ranchero. This would not have been such a singularly important event, had it not been followed by hints of marriage between Judd and Virginia—these sallying forth from not only Judd but from Grayson himself. Virginia was an only child and would one day inherit the ranch, an idea which seemed to delight Judd but to conversely wreak havoc on his young target.

Judd Hazelud had allowed but little of his past to be ferreted out, but Virginia knew with woman's intuition that certain things were not in order. To begin with he was at least 10 years her senior. He was rough and aggressive, although never was seen to touch red liquor, and, though claiming to hail from Texas parentage, he spoke with a distinct Arkansas slang.

Hazelud also claimed to been an expert trainer of horses in the pure western style, but Virginia had taken careful note of the manner in which he once forced a saddle too narrow upon one of her mustangs. The animal had thus been forced into bucking like a rodeo bronc, and had stopped only when beaten into submission by the rope-wielding Judd. That horse had never since been keen to a saddle, but it was upon that moment that Virginia decided she would never allow herself the position of that poor, frightened beast. She never forgot the incident and knew her father would never condone such behavior, were he aware of it.

Thus Virginia was not looking toward Hazelud as a prospective suitor, and it now seemed to the fair, full of self-pity maiden of Ranchero Johnson that she was rapidly approaching a showdown with all parties concerned.

Awaking suddenly from her unconscious state of mind, Virginia purchased several yards of material and said her friendly good-byes to Bell Smithers. She paused at the doorway, suddenly recalling that on this visit to town Judd Hazelud would be waiting for her at the buckboard rather than her father. Virginia was normally accompanied into Kanab by John Grayson, but on this occasion Judd had won out, claiming that he had some important items to purchase for himself and that it would be best if he accompanied the young lady.

A gruff voice met her appearance in the doorway. "Ginny, we got to git now. Climb aboard an' quit laggin'!"

How dare he! Virginia fumed as she approached the wagon, but the heavyset Hazelud was taking delight in the situation.

"What y'a been doin' in thar, buyin' the store! I been waitin' out h'a 'most an hour. Git your self up he'a!"

"Now that's no way to talk to a lady, and that's a fact!" The young rider standing beside his mustang at a nearby hitching post had gone unnoticed until now, but it was evident that he had taken in the scene with much interest and had witnessed enough.

Virginia and Judd pivoted their heads and stared incredulously, each for a different purpose. Virginia had halted beside the buckboard, and suddenly the young man was beside her. He took her hand and gently lifted her to the wagon seat. He took a step backward as Hazelud rose hesitantly. Judd eyed the gun strapped on the younger man's hip and suddenly remember that his own was under the seat. He was also somewhat paralyzed by the thought that he could stand no trouble with the law, and the law was plentiful in Kanab.

Judd spat as he grabbed up the reins, his eyes piercing the newcomer, "Yo'r lucky today, but I'll be seein' ya' agin, ya' nosey young pup!"

Troy stood firm. He had made his decision, and he eyed the larger man carefully as Judd sat down and quickly snapped the reins. The buckboard sped off, but the young lady turned slightly and the wisp of a grin touched her lips . . . It was indeed the young rider she had first noticed when going to the dry-goods store.

CHAPTER 3

AFTER AN EVENTFUL barge crossing of the Colorado River that included a near-drowning of him and another passenger in unseasonably high and fierce water, the Arizona rider fell in with a small cattle drive that was on the northwest trail. Troy O'Neill secured a temporary job with the outfit and spent several days eating dust as drag driver at the right, rear corner of the bawling herd. The prevailing winds made his throat dry as a lime kiln, and the pace was much too slow to suit his needs. Finally, he accepted a pay marker drawn on the Bank of Kanab and headed Sundown to the stage trail, which took a more direct route into Kanab.

Troy knew that Kanab was not known as one of the more corrupt towns of its day, but no doubt remained that it was holding its own as he rode in with the evening haze. He had, however, pictured it as being somewhat of an oasis in the middle of this bleak Utah landscape. It was not that, he realized as he dismounted and wormed his way slowly along the congested, potholed main street where dust choked and impeded the vision of anyone within 20 feet of the ground.

Frock-coated gamblers and crinoline-decked Jezebels promenaded along the boardwalks, while jockeying for position in the street were hunters, trappers and blanketed

Indians. Mexicans with obsidian-black eyes, Mormons with beards, along with miners and leisure-time cowboys bent on treeing the town, and tenderfeet from the East joined these in what seemed a melting pot of noise and perpetual motion.

As he looked in wonder upon the melee, a blaze of red hair above a prim figure caught the corner of his eye. Troy turned to stare in wonderment as the young lady passed close by, and stung by her beauty and green, flashing eyes, he muttered a rather stupid sounding, "Evenin' ma'am," just as she disappeared through a store front. "Well," he muttered aloud but unheard in the chaos of the street, "they certainly aren't all like her. Pretty and proper, that girl!"

Troy led Sundown up the street again, taking in the many stores, noise and confusion. Then he turned back, gravitating toward the spot he had seen the young lady. Here he hitched Sundown to a post and pondered his next move.

Troy scarcely noticed the large, rough-looking individual sitting nearby in the wagon, until an angry outcry from the man attracted his attention and the subsequent encounter . . .

When it was over, Troy watched the buckboard until it disappeared around a corner. Then the youngster's roving but purposeful eyes caught a sign hanging over a large barn:

HAY BURNER
HORSES BOARDED
TEAMS RENTED

There he troughed and quartered Sundown. Then he rented an upstairs room that overlooked the busy street. His final move of the trail was to unpack and remove several layers of alkali dust.

The next morning Troy wandered about several of the numerous establishments. In one place he watched with interest while the faro, poker and roulette croupiers plied their trades, learned from places as distant as the Klondike. It seemed their dress, mannerism and speech also hailed from miles apart.

It was an unequaled scene to the youngster from Arizona, and he finally settled upon watching a poker game at one of the several green-cloaked tables. But two of the beady-eyed card slicks quite unannounced and simultaneously began to cuss out one another, each standing red-faced while throwing accusations about the other fellow's cheating as well as certain birth rights. Cards and cash fell in the wake as the other occupants vacated the table. Suddenly both sallow-faced sharks clawed at their leather, and the older of the two shot the other's eye straight out with a single shot, the younger man spouting life's blood as he flopped dead across Troy's boots. The young rider decided on the moment that he would not wait further and perhaps also impede the passage of a bullet. He went straight to the bank to cash the pay marker he had carried from the trail drive, and immediately thereafter to the general store.

The following August morning was a warm one, as Troy turned eastward from the bustling metropolis of Kanab into the sparse Utah countryside. He carried on the heavy side of 200 pounds of supplies on a newly acquired pack horse, and his poke was next to flat.

The easterly trail was much traveled and worn by riders and wagon wheels, and an easy one for Sundown to follow unassisted. A hazy sun hung high in a dull sky, and eventually Troy became lulled into a dreamy world of thought, talking aloud to himself and the horse through the heat waves that hung over the patches of cholla and mesquite. "Not far to go big boy . . . I hope neither of us gets sun-sick—it's hotter'n a two dollar pistol on the Fourth . . .

Say, she was some lady, eh Sundown? . . . Girls like her—that red hair and those emerald eyes . . . You sure never see that kind diggin' in the gold fields, now do you? Nope. I'll swan if they don't just pop right out of nowhere and then disappear . . . At any rate, you never see 'em again.

According to directions, this haphazard array of sprawling buildings and structures could only be that belonging to the Ranchero Johnson. The young rider wiped the dusty field glass and aimed it eastward again. "Funny looking ranch. Looks more like a town."

The area did appear to have once been a small ranch, but with many years of progressive separation of bunkhouses, barns and dwellings, it eventually had taken on a small town appearance, complete with a wide main street. This street was now framed by dark and old, but seemingly well-kept structures that were scattered about like rising mushrooms.

Troy's glass fell on a large brownstone building. Its features were indefinite, but he judged it to be the main ranch house. It nestled amid a grove of large smoke trees at one end of the street, while a series of corrals festooned in awkward directions from the other.

Motion in the area was almost nil. What did appear was stemming from one of the larger corrals where several figures milled and mixed with horses, most of the time lost in the swirling dust.

Troy touched the mustang with light knee pressure. "All right, Sundown. Last rest before the big ride. Let's make whatever we can of it." The mustang needed no prodding and parted the grama grass in a steady trot, with the pack animal following reluctantly at its heels.

Beyond his studies, Troy O'Neill's younger life had been entirely consumed with duties required of a horse ranch. Thus as he approached this scene he was thoroughly captivated with the action within the large corral. For there, a hapless rider was obviously attempting the record for most times thrown from one bronc. That cowboy would suddenly flop high in the air scarecrow-like fashion, then plunge to the ground in a cloud of alkali. Seconds later he would miraculously clamber aboard the same gray mustang's back, only to be flung crazily into space once again . . . and there seemed something strangely familiar about the individual.

In his approach, Troy could now clearly see that the rider was also spurring and rope-whipping the horse. "Long on animosity, but short on brains," he muttered half aloud, reining up alongside the fence. He was as yet unseen by either the would-be bronc buster or his puppet cowhand, who ran hither and yon in an effort to help while taking the other's oath-filled instructions in perfect stride.

The longer he observed, the angrier Troy became. Finally unable to contain himself longer, he spoke out with a vitreous ring—just as the cowboy picked himself up from what would surely be his final attempt.

"What is it you're trying to do to that animal?" His voice carried over the retreating hoof beats of the gray, momentarily startled. Clearly now this was the same man he had challenged in Kanab, and that individual was scowling redoubtably at this new comer, both hands knuckled at his hips. "Wal, blow me all to pieces! If'n ain't the pup from Kanab! Jest who are you, anyways!"

Troy replied from the saddle, not stepping down. "Name's O'Neill, from Arizona. We've plenty of broncs down there, an' I've broken enough of 'em to saddle to know that you're shore ruining the heck outa that one! Spurs and a rope won't make an animal that's worth a toot when you're through!"

Sundown side-slipped testily as the big cowboy took several rapid steps toward the fence and spat. "Wal, I'll be a gone goose! Judd Hazelud, foreman of one of the biggest hoss ranches in these parts, has jest been tol' how not ta bust a bronc!"

Hazelud eyed the youngster a'top the big mustang with sarcasm and spat again. "O'Neill is it? Wal tell me, mister O'Neill, jest how youns'd go about bustin' that'n an' a dozen more of his kind?" His eyes snapped from side to side contemptuously as he spoke.

Troy slid from his saddle, cradled the reins over the pommel and then stood eyeball to eyeball over the fence from the fuming Hazelhud. A revelation struck him as he eyed the heavyset figure and its hairy, ham-like fists at closer range. "Has me by at least 30 pounds," he thought, observing to himself. "If this animal starts something, O'Neill, you'll be the gone gosling—he's put together like a pine stump."

Outside attention had evidently been drawn toward this new action and confrontation at the corral. For, in addition to the third cowhand who had positioned himself along the fence to Troy's left, from the corner of his eye he vaguely saw a figure approach and then halt near the small end of the semi-circle.

"Yoon's deaf?" Hazelud interrogated again, taking another threatening step while maintaining the same scowl.

"You say you've more like him?" Troy asked redundantly as he strove for control. "What do you mean 'like him'?"

The foreman stuck a boot on a low fence rail and stroked his stubbled chin as he eyed the youngster steadily. "'Pears y'u ask morn y'u answer." He was losing all cool now and he flicked his eyebrows upward in a questioning manner that was all his own. "Reckon yor a man aboot hosses, do y'u?"

"Born an' raised on a hoss ranch down by the Arizona gold fields—I've sit down on more than a few of 'em . . . I also can tell you that if you've even a handful of critters like that gray you'll likely entertain a picnic breakin' 'em. I've seen that type before—'an up close!"

Hazelud looked momentarily as though he would turn aside, changed his mind, and instead rasped poignantly, "Y'u can git straight on yor way, rider, afore I thump your head like a melon ta see if'n it's ripe!"

Troy replied all too simply, "Now you do look like an ornery critter, for a fact!"

That was Judd's cue and he made a threatening dive to climb the fence, but his hostility was frozen suddenly by a piercing voice that was closing fast upon the would-be combatants. "Cool off, Judd! We'll have no thumpin' anyone's head around here jest now!"

The young rider turned to take stock of this newcomer. He was close to the age of Troy's own father, and his leathery face was set with huge, penetrating eyes that seemed to smile when the lips weren't really intending it. He stood tall and heavyset, in plain broadcloth shirt and worn butternut trousers, but holding an air of authority that spoke of his position here. A large, scaly hand was thrust through the fence at Troy. "I'm John Grayson. This is my ranch—the wild one here's my foreman, Judd Hazelud."

Troy introduced himself as he briefly pumped the extended hand, thinking himself fortunate indeed for the interruption.

Grayson ignored the befuddled Hazelud and continued, "Heard y'u say y'u forked animals like that gray a'fore. That so?"

"It's a fact." Troy's sweeping hand indicated the horse in question, now stomping wild and lathered near the corral gate. "He's one of a special breed. I've seen that kind buck down the best riders Arizona has to offer. Only one way that works sure on'em." His voice trailed off as he studied John

Grayson's face, the latter having removed his hat and now standing with a sleeve to his dripping brow.

Thus ignored in this swing of conversation, Grayson's foreman began to back off slowly, muttering something or other concerning other chores under his breath.

Grayson leaned on the fence and looked at Troy, the red mustang and the laden pack animal over with a practiced eye. He said simply, not looking toward his foreman, "Pay not much heed to Judd. Sometimes he takes on the awful manners of a gun-totin' fool." Then, with an offhand gesture toward the pack horse, "Y'u appear to be headin' on a lengthy journey, Mister O'Neill."

Troy answered thoughtfully but in a matter-of-fact manner, "I am. Headin' for a canyon north of here. I've read of some archeological finds there . . . . Sort of a hobby of mine. Been studying it since I was a boy—afraid I'm still an amateur though, at that."

Grayson remained taciturn for a moment, then said, "Well now, each of us follows some sort of star, or whatever—yours jest could be hangin' over that canyon somewhere. But, archi—or whatever, if'n yo'r as good with hosses and broncs as y'u claim, I'd shore pay y'u well to stow them supplies, make yourself real homely-like for a week or so an' help out with those wild critters I jest got in." He pointed his battered felt hat in the direction of the gray that Hazelud and his puppet were now hazing into another corral. Then he returned to eye the youngster carefully. "How's $2 a day sound to y'u?"

Troy reflect this offer with eyebrows upraised. Two dollars a day was a goodly amount, and the supplies at Kanab had taken nearly all his resources. On the other hand, he was upon the last leg of a journey that really needed no interruptions . . . Then he looked beyond John Grayson and squarely into the greenest eyes he had seen in less than two days.

The young lady stared back and smiled slightly, making it quite obvious that she remembered this rider. Auburn hair curled and streamed out behind her hat as it was touched lightly by the wind. Her smooth, cream-colored skin was offset by a green neckerchief, and she stood relaxed in black riding clothes that seemed to accentuate her superb, young lines . . . The same girl! Troy was lost for words and stared boyishly.

Grayson realized suddenly that his daughter had pre-empted their conversation with her appearance, and he continued with instruction. "This here's my daughter Virginia. Ginny, this young rider says he's Mister O'Neill from down Arizona way—man of sorts with hosses, so he sez. I jest invited him ta stay a spell an' help break that wild herd."

Virginia stepped around her father to extend an ungloved hand, looking upward into Troy's face. "I'm very pleased to make acquaintance, Mister O'Neill . . . Will you be staying?"

The young rider dropped the reins he had been clutching and took the small, extended hand in his own. Its warmth seemed to permeate every dendrite in his hand, and looking into her soft, green eyes he found no sudden desire to hurry upon his way. He would stay indeed—if only for a short while. "I'm Troy O'Neill," he forced out. "My father's name is Mister O'Neill."

The young lady of the Ranchero Johnson giggled at this untimed bit of humor. Then she politely withdrew her hand, her face flushed with a pleasing smile.

CHAPTER 4

TROY'S METHOD for breaking the mustangs worked almost without fail, but was one requiring much teamwork, concentration and considerable effort.

It first required that he single out a good snubbing horse, which he did along with the reluctant Huzelud and one of Grayson's top hands. They then would rope one of the wild broncs, and halter him and snub him to the snubbing horse, drawing him up tight to the saddle horn. Troy then had Hazelud swing his saddle up to him, and this he carefully eased down onto the bronc's back. Then he had Judd reach under the bronc and with a wire hook catch the cinch and pull it to the left side. Troy then reached over with another wire, snagged the cinch and proceeded to cinch the saddle down on the wild mustang. He then eased backward out of his saddle and sat on the snubbing horse's rump. Then the other hand mounted in front of him and nudged their animal up a few steps to pull the bronc alongside, where Troy would ease over onto the wild one.

Upon mounting the bronc he had the hand drag the two around the corral several times and then hand him the snubbing line. At this time he tucked the snub rope into his belt and proceeded to ride the mustang around the corral several times, and hence out onto the prairie for an hour or so.

To dismount, he had the hand pick up the bronc, then he would slide back onto the snubbing horse and off to unsaddle the bronc.

Once or twice through the procedure seemed all that was necessary to break each mustang. In this slow methodical way, three cowhands were able to tame at least one horse per day—two on a good day.

Troy's first three days on the Ranchero Johnson were exhausted in a like manner, and aside from the scornful contempt constantly emanating from Judd, the young rider was thoroughly enjoying this unplanned adventure.

His spirits were further uplifted upon the several occasions he thought he spied Virginia looking on from a distance, or glancing his way upon a return from one of her infrequent rides into the southern prairie. But she did not approach him, and in fact her game was to quickly disappear whenever he attempted the most remote move in her general direction.

The rider's evenings were consumed over his archaeological books and maps. He had discovered an old picnic table behind one of the small bunkhouses. Here he scanned maps and re-read those items of particular interest to his quest. One such evening he glanced up to discover Virginia standing nearby. She eyed him and the paraphernalia on the table questioningly. Then her green eyes suddenly widened and sparkled, while a luminous smile flashed over her attractive face.

"Father was right—you really do study a lot of books and things. Why, that book is a Bible . . . I didn't know you were a Bible-toting cowboy."

Virginia paused as she scanned the other items scattered about the table. "What are these books? And those are maps, aren't they?"

Then Virginia noticed Troy's questioning look, fixed on his face since the "Bible-toting" remark. She bubbled quickly, "I'm sorry. I didn't mean anything bad by that remark concerning your Bible . . . Actually, it's refreshing to see someone use one for something besides the decoration of a library table. You do have me wondering about these other things, though. Why do you have all those maps?"

Troy was still trying to overcome the initial surprise of Virginia's presence. "They're maps of Indian territory and books on archaeology that I'm studying. I've been interested in it for several years." He started to rise but she waved him down and took a seat opposite on a bench. He squirmed uncomfortably and repositioned himself, never taking his eyes off her.

The young lady of the ranchero swung into an easy subject change. "You certainly have a way with the mustangs, Troy O'Neill," she said with a smile. "That Judd! Why, he would still be out there whipping the first one if you hadn't come along and interfered . . . You admire horses, don't you?"

"I certainly do. Started training my first colt when I as 8 and he was 2 months old." He hesitated, a small amount of anxiety taking hold as he looked at her lips and back into the emerald eyes again.

Virginia was likewise returning the interest in the young rider with her own thoughts. In him she saw not only someone her own age, but also one who was interesting, knowledgeable, and one who too was searching for adventure in life. Also, this man was much more handsome than was Judd or any of the host of young men with groping hands that she was used to encountering at the Kanab dances. She arrested her reflective mood and removed her hat and riding gloves, while repositioning herself sideways on the bench. She said, "I wish you had been here to train some of my colts. Judd tried that too of course, but he took them out too young—ruined several of them. I think he is prone to take out his frustrations or—or something, on horses.

Troy placed a book aside and leaned back against a smoke tree. "How old were they?"

"He tried riding them before they were yearlings."

"That's too soon. A foal should be haltered and led around some—works pretty good with a soft rope around the girth an' run through the halter. But a yearling shore can't carry much weight—certainly not a full-grown rider like Judd." The talker paused to contemplate his listener, then continued, "How they're worked in the first months'l stay with 'em forever. Dad tried to make me wait 'til they were 3 before sittin' 'em, but I found that if I started 'em slow at 2 years old I'd get a gentler horse—that is, if I trained 'em right." He halted, realizing that he was rambling on about something this young lady probably already knew. His heart was pounding like a jackrabbit's.

Virginia was definitely interested, and in everything this young man had to say. She took the opportunity to revert to her original question. "Are you studying to be a prospector?"

Troy grinned and replied, "Not really. I was schooled in many subjects by my mother. One that I like best is archaeology—she sent for books on it from the university back in New York, and I've been reading them several years. I've a lot to learn, though . . . Anyway, it's a science dealing with the recovery of objects, and the understanding of people who owned and used them in years past. Artifacts, we can call them. Such items can be dated and studied, such as ancient tools, weapons, or objects of daily use. And sometimes they're also worth a lot of money." Troy broke off, though, and then continued, "No. I'm not going to be a prospector—at least not as you put it. My father and uncle Jim were for a time, or at least they fancied themselves they were. That's how we all wound up in the Arizona gold fields . . . Father's ranching now and my mother passed on awhile back. Uncle Jim, he was the real wanderer in the family."

Virginia's eyes lit up as she exclaimed enigmatically, "Jim O'Neill! Your uncle?" A hand shot to her lips in a gesture of surprise, and she paled ever so slightly. "Your uncle?" she repeated.

Troy looked at her with disbelieve. "You've heard of my uncle?"

Virginia's reply came quickly. "Yes, if he's the same man. A man by that name stopped here at the ranchero for supplies over a year ago. An older man—only stayed a day and then headed north. My father said he was looney, or something to that effect, and tried to talk him out of going up there. He didn't succeed, and we haven't seen him since . . . My goodness, your uncle!"

"Yes, that had to be him all right. We surmised he might have gone back for the treas . . ."

"Treasure! Oh gracious, the treasure! Not you too!" Virginia Grayson suddenly stopped and then giggled without restraint.

"What's so funny about it?"

"That's a silly old Paiute legend that's been around for at least 100 years. The Indians have told stories about a treasure hidden in a large canyon to the north." She paused.

"Your uncle wasn't serious, was he?"

Almost without thinking, Troy blurted, "He was serious all right: I have a map and notes that he made—he said they'd lead me to its location . . . He was very close to it himself, once many years ago. Said he didn't see it, but knew it was the spot just the same." Troy stopped as Virginia's eyes mocked him. Then with a sudden realization, he continued thoughtfully, "Besides, if what you say is true, then my uncle would be a liar—." He interrupted himself with the all-too painful reflection that Jim O'Neill had indeed been known to rubberize the truth about many of his Quixotic adventures.

Virginia suddenly reached out to touch Troy's hand. "My father is certain that the legend of such treasure is either grossly exaggerated or completely manufactured."

"At that, there's still the matter of my uncle. If he left here a year ago and hasn't returned, then I will try to find him . . . Whether he lied about a treasure, or didn't."

Virginia said nothing for a long moment, then sighed with resignation, "Well, if you're in need of a second opinion other than my father's, I'll get Tecao to tell you about the legends of the northern canyons."

"Tee-what? . . . Who's that?"

Virginia spelled out the name and then said, "It's pronounced, 'Tee-coo,' with long e's and o's. He's one of the older Indians in my father's employ. None of us really knows his age, but he is still very strong and an excellent horseman. Grew up among the Paiute and other Indian tribes. In fact, he lived in one of those northern canyons as a young boy—perhaps the very one you talk of. Most certainly he's an expert on the area and its various tales . . . There are others you know—I mean besides stories of a hidden treasure."

Troy's interest was revitalized. "What others?"

Virginia merely said, "I'll let Tecao explain. And when he does, I trust you'll change your mind about going."

This amazing and beautiful young lady of the ranchero had not removed her hand from its rest on Troy's, and the young rider now felt its heat clear to his trembling knees. He looked at her fully now, and thought her indeed beautiful! "OK. I'll meet with this Indian as soon as you can take me to him, and gladly. But I rather doubt that he'll influence my feelings. I'm still concerned for my uncle—and as for the treasure—well, I'm not so easily convinced that it's just some story."

Both youngsters were suddenly conscious of the approach of a third party, and looked up to see Judd stalking toward them from one of the barns. Virginia hesitatingly but deliberately withdrew her hand as Hazelud approached the table. He glared at the girl while showing an obvious and total disregard for Troy's presence.

"Ginny, I've tol' y'u a'fore—yo'r ta stay away from these drifters an' cowhands wanderin' through har!" He then looked vehemently at Troy and snorted poignantly, "An' particular with the likes o'him!"

Virginia's face turned almost the color of her hair. Troy rose abruptly, but for the second time she waved him down. She in turn rose and faced the obnoxious cowhand. Livid with anger, she suddenly poked a finger in the foreman's face, waving it in disgust.

"That is absolutely the last straw, Judd Hazelud! You've no right to be telling me anything! I'm not yours to boss around, and neither is this ranch—not yet it isn't! This place is my father's, my mother's and . . . mine! And I belong to me! I don't care one hoot what father may have told you about protecting me, and I don't need nor want your type of protection! I'm of an age to make my own decisions, and one of those is for you to henceforth stay completely away from me! . . . And while you're about it, please stay away from my friends!" She stopped short and glared at her target with contempt.

Judd had backed away from the onslaught, and now he wheeled and stomped about in a small circle as if pondering the situation or some reply. No idea came, however, and he suddenly turned to stomp off toward the ranch house, kicking at the needle grass in unmitigated retreat.

The young lady of the Ranchero Johnson suddenly turned bright, laughing eyes to Troy. "Oh," she giggled without restraint, "I have wanted to tell that cowboy off for such a long time! And . . . now I've done it. Oh, I'm just tickled pink!"

Troy asked with wonderment, regaining his feet, "But I thought you and he were friends . . . Then—then you don't lov . . . (ve) . . . like him?"

"Like? I can't stand that rude, despicable man. The only friendship ever between us was in his own conceited imagination. I've just been dying to tell him off!" Then her look turned to one of consternation, with eyes no longer laughing and her lips straightened in line. "Now—now, he may turn on you. Oh, I'm afraid I have been thinking only of myself. Judd is the type to do something reckless."

Troy was overcome by her show of compassion. He retrieved her hand, holding it lightly in his own as he spoke firmly and with a feeling he had not known before. "You needn't be concerned for my sake. I'm big enough to handle Judd if he starts anything. And if he ever bothers you again, he's going to have to answer to me!"

The young lady returned his stare, then blushed noticeably as she said, "Thank you, Troy O'Neill." Then she carefully withdrew her hand and turned to walk toward the house.

The young rider gazed after her and only when she had left his view did he begin gathering up the materials on the table. The last item, his Bible, he picked up and fingered its worn leather cover thoughtfully before placing it carefully in the open saddlebag.

CHAPTER 5

THE PRESENT DAYS at the ranchero were not passing in a positive manner for Judd Hazelud. Outwardly, he continued to perform his duties as foreman of the ranch, but inwardly he had become lost in a maze of self-pity and bitterness.

The man's long-range plans had suddenly been turned to shambles by this opponent, Troy O'Neill. His dream of one day owning the affections of Virginia, along with that of controlling the Johnson spread, were blowing away like trail dust. This newcomer had found favor in the ranch owner as well as the other ranch hands by his knowledge and ability with stock, whereas Judd had been relegated aside by such horsemanship and applied knowledge.

Judd had seen Troy and Virginia in company upon several occasions since that first encounter, had been privy to their longing looks at one another, and had been subjected to fitful nightmares of the two in each other's arms.

Now Judd's envious thoughts turned to those of revenge. At first he had merely wanted to vindicate himself with Virginia—but that seemed next to impossible now. He also had wanted to maintain his position on the ranch—now, with that rider around this too suddenly seemed impossible, or unlikely at the least . . . Just one person stood at the apex of his problems, and he must find a way to rid himself of that menace.

It had been a long, hard and uphill trail for Hazelud, and he had wandered many miles from Pine Bluff back in the Arkansas River country. Pine Bluff . . . His chest sagged suddenly and a long-dammed exhale burst through his lips into the darkness as he thought about his home of long ago.

Judd wore his 32 years well and could remember vividly that day, 14 years earlier, when he had been hurriedly forced to leave—no, escape, Pine Bluff. There he had shot and killed another young man in a foolish, dance-hall fight. Drunk on moonshine, he had retained enough of his faculties to realize his peril. He had needlessly gunned down another human and, drunk or sober, would be sought by the local sheriff. In fact, he figured his fate would be that of a hanging were he captured. He remembered the blurry farewell to his mother and sisters, and how he had launched himself into the hills like a hunted animal.

Judd had no formal education and had sought no communication with his family over these 14 years. And somehow those years had passed—with his staying alive but always in a state of wandering and fluidity. Ever graduating westward, he had lived not with brainpower but rather by his own muscle and the gun. Years of running bad, riding the ragged edge of capture with bands of rustlers and other outlaws on the dodge, had formed a hard and calloused shell about him . . . He had played the role of the law only on one occasion—that gratuity which had led to his employment on Grayson's ranch—and that occasion hadn't been a matter of choice. He guessed he hadn't any choice now, either.

Killing this adversary certainly would not vindicate him in Virginia's or Grayson's eyes—unless he could perform the act without arrest. This seemed unlikely; still, his animal-like instinct told him any move he made must be drastic. Inwardly, he fought with this . . . He had killed before and knew its consequences.

The sound of hoof beats on the down-trail caused him to quicken and peer through the dusk of evening. He leaned backward, melting into the shadow of the huge saguaro as he slipped the six-gun from its holster. For time immemorial, men had hated and even killed one another over their women. He had seen his enemy ride this trail and knew he would return. This would be Judd's moment, and at this he would win . . .

THIS INDIAN was unlike any Troy had ever seen or heard of. The bronze figure stood nearly six-and-a-half-foot, was decked in clean buckskin that contained few frills and wore a tan leather hat in true, western style. On his feet were riding boots of the finest leather, and huge, ornamented rowels decorated his spurs. As if this were not impressive enough, tied low on his hips were two six-guns, hanging from a single belt but in cross-draw style. His obsidian eyes were like holes carved into high cheek bones, and at this moment they bore into Troy over a hook nose that made the young rider think of peering squarely into the face of an eagle.

The aging Indian was one of Grayson's most trusted employees. And, as was his want, he had been allowed to construct a thatched lean-to of his own under the canyon wall a short ride from the main ranch. Here he had maintained a certain privacy, coming and going at his own bidding for as many years as most of the ranch hands could recall. On occasion he had been away several months at a time, always to return. In more recent years his sudden, unannounced escapes—supposed by most to be returns to his people or one of his tribes—became less frequent. At this point, Tecao had not strayed from the ranch for the better part of a year, and had in fact returned from that latest sojourn to remain sullen and taciturn for many weeks, which led others to speculate that some tragedy may have befallen his family, or at least a circumstance of some shattering proportions. He was a proud individual and rarely offered explanations of any sort to those who dared question him.

After her brief introduction, Virginia stood in the background and watched as the two sized each other up rooster-like. She had arranged this meeting in the face of sizable protest from Tecao, who had agreed only after lengthy pleadings and an explanation of Troy's concern for a lost uncle.

It was the Indian who broke the ice, giving Troy a momentary surprise as he spoke out simply, but in near-perfect English. "I have watched you. You are a good man with the horses." His lips cracked with just the wisp of a grin and he continued, "You did show Judd a trick or so."

Tecao extended a hand, which Troy reached for eagerly. The young rider's hands were sizable, but the Indian engulfed his in a swoop and pressed it firmly.

"You're certainly not—well, not quite . . ."

". . . what you thought of me," the Indian finished. "Come." He led the way to several crude benches that rested alongside the lean-to.

Once seated, the old Indian pointed toward the western wall of the canyon. "Look," he said slowly, "the sun is setting at this time . . . I watch it every evening. But for the life-giving light and strength of the morning, it is more wonderful than any sunrise can be . . . A satisfying sight, and a time for looking into one's self, or into the soul of another. It is the time to think and to make plans . . . Let us look before we talk."

Troy and Virginia did look, and both were captured as the sun's golden rays shimmered and seemed to slice into a thousand tiny needles that bounced off the distant, jagged rampart. The spell lasted but a few moments, but it was indeed a sight worth watching, being further enhanced and contrasted by the deep blue sky above and the purple walls below. In this memorable moment, Troy stole a glance at his young companion. The sun's final rays had turned her hair to a fire-red hue. "She is more beautiful," he thought, "than any sunset could ever be!"

"You wish to go in search of your uncle?" The question was flung suddenly and directly to the point.

Troy responded in like fashion. "Not entirely. That is, I was really searching for him when I came here to the ranch. But, now that I know he's been here—gone north and not returned—well, now I feel an obligation to try and locate him."

"That is a desolate area, up in the canyons. Do you know his reason for going there?"

Troy suddenly knew that the Indian already had the answer to that question. He had also begun answering Tecao somewhat evasively, and recognized that his chances for help from that wise one would be nil if he didn't change directions.

"Yes, I believe I know. He was trying to return to a particular canyon—one he had stumbled across about 20 years ago. Truth is, he claimed that he and another prospector had been near to something—something that could be buried treasure, or so they reckoned. But his partner came up missing, and Uncle Jim found his pard's severed head—placed during the night on a shelf, and near to a sealed cave mouth. Anyway, he became scared for his own life and fled from the canyon . . . As far as I know, this is the only time he's been back."

The Indian's ebony eyes flashed momentarily, as though a revelation had struck him, then he altered the feeling and merely asked, "This canyon. Did he tell you what it looked like?"

"He said that it was huge—not as large, certainly, as the Grand, but still big, open on one end and deep on the other. Sounded sort of like a huge amphitheatre, and filled with large sandstone spires."

The Indian uttered something low and unintelligible as he turned slightly and gazed off toward one of the distant buttes. Still looking away, he queried, "What was this buried treasure your uncle spoke of?"

"He didn't know exactly what it was. His partner had found a link of gold bracelet with several jewels in it, and near that same spot they discovered a small trail that led upward along the canyon wall. Then the other prospector met his death . . . . I've studied the history of that area, and I believe there just could be an old Spanish treasure cached there."

The Indian had remained as still as a rock, and now tore his eyes from the distance to cast them upon the young rider once more. "Wisdom comes with the years, just as certainly as many things appear pretty and shiny, and are yet totally worthless . . . Virginia says you have studied the ways of the earth and its people of past ages. She informed you of your uncle's return to that canyon, so you were not just wandering around in search of him when you came here. You came to search for a treasure."

Troy brimmed his hat nervously in his fingers. He glanced first at Virginia and then faced the Indian squarely. "Yes, I started out to find a treasure. Perhaps one that doesn't even exist. Virginia claims it to be an old wife's tale, and Mister Grayson says it's an outright lie . . . Even so, I'd like the chance to explore that canyon some, and to look for my uncle, if he still lives. As everyone saw when I came here, I've prepared pretty well for the trip—spent my whole shebang on supplies enough for two trips, in fact!"

Virginia broke her silence for the first time since she had introduced the pair. "Tecao, perhaps you should inform our young and daring rider of the other superstitions concerning that canyon, since he seems bent to go up there."

The Indian smiled at her concern for this young man, then his face hardened once more. "There are other facts—not just superstitions." He became taciturn for the moment as he began somewhat absently to draw figures in the sand with a stick. Then he said, "A small band of my people still live in that canyon. They are the old Aztecan tribe—few in number now, and ravaged by many diseases. For as long as they know, they have survived in that bitter area. Our so-called brothers, the Paiute, have waged a somewhat successful war on us for many years, up and around the canyon's rim.

Troy said apprehensively, "You talk as though you really are one of the canyon people."

The old man showed no outward hint of anger at this interrogation. Rather, he continued, "I was one of those people. I left the canyon to explore the outside world when very young—to seek, perhaps as you do now, adventure and a new life. I lived among white men and Paiute alike for many years, and have lived here at the ranchero for perhaps 29 or more seasons . . . A year past, I returned to my people. And that time I found them nearly destroyed by disease and killings. While there I led a hunting party above the canyon, and we were again attacked by the Paiute. In that venture, I was not lucky." He had loosened a buckskin tie while speaking, and now pulled his shirt aside to reveal a jagged scar on his right breast.

Virginia became emotional. "Oh dear God! That is why you remained alone upon your return! You were wounded, and—and you should have let me know. I would have helped you!"

"I was struck, but as you see, I have survived. But that is why I have taken much practice with these guns I now wear." He paused momentarily and then said, "But there is something else—and that is a fact. I will return to the canyon once more, perhaps soon, but it will be to die there."

Troy and his young companion were captured by this latest, suspense-filled statement. "Why?" they asked simultaneously.

"I have thought much about it. I am old, and my remaining sunsets must be few in number. It is my home, and I feel certain that I will die there . . . I will return some day—perhaps soon." Then, almost desultorily, he added with sternness. "I will do that alone!"

Troy gained his feet rapidly and proclaimed, "No! We will go together, you and I!"

The Indian eyed the young man with more than common curiosity, then turned to speak softly to the girl. "Miss Ginny, if you care at all for this Arizona rider you cannot let him go—not for a treasure, or for his uncle." He paused, then continued hoarsely, "I have not told you of yet another legend of that canyon. Many have found it—white men and Indian alike—and have gone in. Those few who escaped to return a second time, well, those were never heard from again. Young rider, it is certain that your uncle has joined his partner. The canyon casts a bad omen on second visits—it always has."

As his voice trailed off, the Indian looked through the dimming evening light at the two young people. Virginia had at one point taken Troy's hand, and now clung wide-eyed to him. Troy seemed almost not to notice the girl as he stared down at Tecao's etchings in the dirt. Then he drew himself up.

"TECAO DREW FIGURES IN THE SAND — THE SAME TRAIL MARKERS THAT LED MY UNCLE INTO THE CANYON AND TO THE TREASURE!"

"Uncle Jim dead? Maybe so, and just maybe not . . . What about the treasure? Does that exist?

The Indian replied strongly, "I cannot say. Miss Virginia says you study the white man's good book. I think that would be a better thing to follow than a trail to nowhere. I speak the truth, and you will find that truth is an absolute habit of mine!" He rose from the bench suddenly, turned, and stood unmoving toward the east. It was an obvious ending to this encounter.

The youngsters had taken the precaution of riding out separately, but they would return together under cover of the evening's haze. They waved warmly to Tecao from their saddles. The old Indian gestured off-handedly, then turned to disappear through the door of his lean-to.

When they were out of earshot and sight of the cabin, Troy drew rein and motioned for Virginia to do likewise. Forcing Sundown close to her black, he spoke excitedly. "Ginny, my uncle was not a liar. He found something in that canyon, and . . ."

"Troy, how can you be so certain?" she interrupted with a show of impatience, drawing tightly on the reins.

"Tecao himself told me, without know it. While he talked he drew figures in the sand. I saw them—the same bird designs my uncle sketched in his notes. The same trail marker that led him into the canyon and to the treasure!"

"Oh, Troy O'Neill, but you are stubborn!" Virginia proclaimed passionately. "You will go and get your own head chopped off! Well—well, if that's what you want, then just go ahead! I don't care!" She spurred the black, and horse and rider disappeared rapidly down the darkened trail.

Troy hesitated a moment, captivated by a sudden realization . . . There was more than a treasure to think of now—this beautiful, wonderful girl! She did care, and cared a great deal! He was overwhelmed at the thought that perhaps she could be his own. Unhoped for! . . . He rode unconsciously through the darkness toward the ranchero, his mind's eye flitting from the triangular bird signs to Virginia's angered, passionate, green eyes.

CHAPTER 6

JUDD STEPPED from behind the huge saguaro and faced the uphill trail. Hoof beats rang ominously now and the horse and rider bearing down on him were becoming visible through the evening light. He kept the gun low, but lifted its barrel in line with the approaching rider . . . A sudden fear caught him and he decided at the last split moment that he would not kill his enemy—not this time, at least. He would first put the fear of God in him and perhaps send him on his way. Later, if this proved unsuccessful . . .

The black mustang snorted loudly as it sensed an unknown presence. Then the Colt exploded in Judd's hand as the animal reared, taking the full force of the bullet in its neck.

The stricken horse was falling backward as Virginia's scream rent the air. She was pitched violently toward the animal and then flung backward and over its side.

Hazelud realized his error in gross, petrified horror. "No! Oh no! Ginny! Y'u—y'u." He ran toward her unmoving form, half hidden by her black horse, which was now making huge, wheezing hopeless efforts to regain its feet. So complete was Judd's horror that he was totally unaware of the second rider's full-tilt approach, and of the form that now hurtled upon him in aerial assault.

There was a ripping of cloth, a rasping and tearing of spurs on flesh, and a gasping cry as the weight of Troy's body landed full force on Judd's huge frame. Sundown plunged snorting down the trail in fright, empty stirrups flapping, as the two forms rolled and parted.

Judd's gun had sailed high and away, and now he made a gasping, winded effort to regain his feet and senses.

"Curse you, Judd!" Troy groped his way upward and into a crouch, then launched his body again toward the disoriented, hazy figure before him. "Y'u done it now . . . Y'u shot her!"

Virginia regained enough of her faculties to make a weak and stupefied attempt to rise. Then she felt a numbness and terror, and she faltered, her heart throbbing like a drum. She attempted to speak, to scream out if possible, but a sickening sensation put her head in a spin, and finally she lay again unconscious on the ground.

Judd hadn't recovered fully as the whirling, Tasmanian devil-like form was once more upon him. Troy felt his numb fists strike the flesh and bone of his adversary's face as his piston arms whirled continuously. Then he was cast violently groundward by an unexpected thrust of Judd's powerful legs.

The Arizona rider groped about in search of a club, a rock—a weapon of any kind. He found only sand, pebbles and dead mesquite twigs. His muscle, flesh and very bones seemed to develop their own savage emotions . . . Judd Hazelud had shot and killed Virginia! A lightning fire and fury controlled his every emotion. He loved this young lady of the ranchero, and she was dead! Dead at the hands of this animal before him. By all things holy, he would himself become a killer! Death was manifest within him, and he clawed for a gun which was not there. Mind and muscle

contracted and burst forth again. This time he moved aside like a cat, to reach Judd from behind and coil an arm around the thick neck like a snake. Closing tightly around the muscular bulge, he jerked backward, bringing Judd's body along in a gasping, clutching effort to break the vise. Then Hazelud thrust himself backward and fell heavily upon Troy, rolling then to the side in readiness to strike back. His hand felt the touch of cold steel. The gun! He quickly gained his feet, coming about with the gun barrel glinting as it trembled in Troy's direction in the moonlight.

"Yo'r to be the dead one!" Hazelud spat. The foaming blood frothed from his mouth as he half stumbled toward his victim. He advanced without fear, knowing that this time he would indeed kill this rider, and a faint, grotesque smile tried to part the blood and welts that had become his face. His fingers closed tighter at the same instant the roar of a Winchester shook the small clearing. His body danced backward as the bullet smashed his gun hand and thudded into his shoulder. Pieces of the exploding six-gun spattered across his body, and he drew rigid, crying out in mortal fear and pain.

John Grayson made a flying dismount amid the melee to tower menacingly over his moaning foreman. "By Judas, yo'r not kilt—but y'u won't be killin' no one else around here either!

"Didn't try to kill no one," Hazelud whined from a cowering position, "Jest wanted ta scare 'im!" He half pointed toward Troy with his good, left hand. He started to rise in a pleading manner toward John Grayson, but the owner, seeing the control of his foreman, turned in a wild mood toward Troy, who now stood looking on in total disarray.

"What's going on here O'Neill?"

Grayson's answer came by way of a faltering, stumbling ball of emotion, as Virginia reached her father to fling herself about his neck. "Father!" . . . He nearly killed me . . . And—he shot Minnie!" Her voice cracked and fell into sobs.

Love and happiness filled Troy at the sight of Virginia. Then the young rider moved several steps closer to John Grayson. "He did sir—shot her black from ambush. I'd bet though, that he was trying to get me . . . An'—an', I thought he had shot Ginny. Lord, he must have gone plumb loco!"

Grayson took in the total situation with a deep breath, and his attention now focused venomously upon the cowering, whining figure of Hazelud. "By Judas," he roared again. "Judd, yo'r done about here! We'll patch y'u up and get y'u into Kanab tomorrow, but I shore won't have y'u on this ranch no more! Savvy? . . . Now, git to yo'r hoss an' follow us—if y'u can—and if y'u can't—well, then that's OK with me!

Emotions had run so intently that no one seemed to notice the tall, grim figure that melted backward into the shadows toward the blackness of the canyon wall. It was the image of one who now knew what must be done—as one with eyes that seemingly pierced the future as well as the darkness of this night.

Mid-morning saw a heavily bandaged figure unceremoniously vacate the Ranchero Johnson, hunched over in a buckboard and escorted by one of Grayson's most trusted hands. John Grayson and his wife Martha, along with Troy and Virginia, all peered after the wagon until it rolled out of sight amid a cloud of dust along the huge rampart that marked the western canyon wall.

Grayson turned suddenly to affix questioning eyes upon his daughter. "Ginny, what in the world riled Judd ta sech action? I'm asking an' I want to know, cause I gotta toss y'u a hunch that he's so riled up—well, he may be back . . . I'd like to know what his game is."

Virginia's face colored suddenly and she was momentarily at a disadvantage for words.

Troy's spurs clinked on the porch floorboards as he stepped forward. "Sir. Perhaps I should be the one to answer that. I'm right sorry, but—but Judd, well he was jealous of me. At least I think so . . . Truth is, he wanted to marry your daughter an' he thought . . ."

"He thought I loved him!" Virginia interrupted Troy. "Well, I didn't—and I never would have married Judd . . . He—he was unkind, weak-charactered, and—stupid, too!"

The young lady of the ranchero now turned to her parents passionately. "Oh, father—mother, I know you both thought him to be all right, but he never was my preference. It became so that he thought he owned me. He saw Troy and me together several times and it—well, it infuriated him something awful. Well, I told him that I didn't belong to him and that he was not going to be my boss."

"Uh-huh!" acknowledged her father. He gripped his pipe and held it carefully away from his lips, eyeing Troy with a new intensity. "And then, young man, just what were you two up to that time of night on the canyon trail."

"Why John! John Grayson!" It was the first show of emotion from the rancher's wife, and now she faced her husband with a quick show of fearlessness. "These two youngsters don't need our permission—to go riding . . . Besides," she looked protectively at her daughter, "I trust Virginia. And this young man, well I think he's been good for her—a little more deering-do than she's used to, but what's the harm in that?"

It had been more than a mild statement from his sometimes mousey wife, and John Grayson's face broke slowly into a grin, as he eyed her not unlike a treed cowboy. "Aw, Marty. I didn't mean . . ." Troy stepped forward again, saying resolutely, "Mister Grayson, I'll explain what we were doing out in the canyon last night." Troy then launched into the episode, beginning with his true reason for coming by the Johnson ranch: of his studies in archaeology and his uncle's story and map which could hold promise of untold treasure; of Virginia's concern and her request that he meet with Tecao, and finally of the meeting she had arranged between him and the Indian.

The Grayson's had seated themselves and listened intently during the lengthy accounting. Troy closed his story, "You know what happened on the trail back. Worst luck though. I should have went right on with Ginny instead of stopping to think it all over. She was nearly killed because of my foolish act, and I'm truly sorry . . . And Judd. Well, I reckon he for certain would have bored me through if y'u hadn't come along . . ."

Grayson interrupted the rider, his tone low and true. "No. Y'u wouldn't have been kilt. But Judd now that's somethin' else. He'd of died a fate worse than bein' shot if'n I hadn't showed. In fact, he was plumb lucky I winged him. If I'd been a moment later he'd of had a knife buried in his back first off, an' then been slit from ear ta ear with that same weapon!"

"Tecao," Troy breathed out slowly. "I wondered why he didn't show when Judd fired that shot."

Grayson echoed his words. "Show? Why he didn't show? That's a good one, 'cause he showed all right! Was hid away in the shadows. Saw his knife glint as I rode up to the clearing . . . No way would Judd have ever pulled that trigger!"

CHAPTER 7

The Ranchero Johnson
Kanab, Utah Postal
August 12, 1875

Dear Father,

So much has happened since I left our ranch
that I really don't know where to begin, but I
feel a need to write an accounting of some of my
ventures, and also to assure you that I am well. I
hope and trust that both you and the ranch are also
in fine order.

I discovered it a long journey indeed from our
homestead up into the Utah Territory, and I saw
many exciting places along the way—as well as a
few, no, actually more than a few, exciting people
along the path.

Just recently I've accepted a temporary
position as foreman of a spread called the Johnson
Ranchero, from where I now write. I saw the job
is "temporary" as I felt honor-bound to its owner,
John Grayson, to accept it and his need for me at

this time—since he has helped me in a rather unpleasant situation involving his recent foreman.

Your teachings in horsemanship have been invaluable to my present job. I've been breaking and training a bunch of wild mustang colts and 2-year-olds, and the method of breaking them with a snubbing horse—the one you and Uncle Jim showed me years back—it has been especially useful with a particularly wild herd. But the old standby of using soft rawhide hackamore works many of the younger ones just fine.

And, speaking of Uncle Jim, I am afraid that he has indeed returned to his "treasure" canyon. The Graysons have informed me that he stopped here a short while after he left us. That has been about a year past, and he was packing north into Indian country—which I now understand is still a wild and unsettled area. Since he hasn't returned, I now fear the worst may have happened—although it is undoubtable that there are other ways to get out of that area besides this route. Anyway, I intend to go on up to the canyon and make my search as soon as possible. Please don't have alarm at this, as I now believe that I will not be going into the canyon country alone. For it seems I have gained a friendly and persistently protective shadow—an Indian named Tecao, pronounced Tee-Coo, who seems to have taken up homestead beside my every move.

The Indian is an expert shot and has been showing me some tips about shooting, as we have practiced together almost every evening of late. One thing he showed me is how to "point" with a six-gun. And, rude or not, it really works! (And you remember just how bad I used to be!)

Anyway, Tecao is an old man. How old it is difficult to say, as he is strong as an oxen and wiser than most people I've met. He has confided that the canyon in question was once his very home, and that he must return to it soon. I feel that he will take up my quest and travel with me, so I ask that you not concern yourself with my forthcoming adventure. Indeed, I now have two reasons to continue, for I have not lost sight of a treasure or archaeological find as well as my want to seek after uncle Jim.

The Graysons are wonderful people and I have been accepted as one of their own, or almost it seems. I must also confess that I have become very fond of their daughter, Virginia. Ginny is a year or so younger, and is very kind, knowledgeable, and also quite beautiful. I'm certain that she cares not a hoot for my pending venture, as she has voiced that opinion on several occasions—like every day! I confess also that I feel in somewhat of a quandary and at the same time flattered by her apprehension and concern. However, I shall do what I set out to do. I believe I will succeed.

Father, much time will pass before this letter reaches you. My adventure may even be successfully at an end by that time. I will have word to you as soon as I am in a situation to write.

Again, I trust this letter finds you in good health. I read my Bible daily, and I haven't forgotten mother and her wishes.

With love, your son Troy

TROY RAISED his eyes toward the approaching grayness of evening, already casting dense shadows alongside the covert. Then he carefully folded the letter and stuffed it into his vest pocket. The light trickling sound of the creek before him hid the gliding, light footsteps of the figure which suddenly appeared at his side. His buckskin made no noise as it brushed the branches aside, and then Tecao was perched like an eagle on a nearby stump.

"You fish, young rider?" the Indian nodded toward the stream.

Troy smiled at the thought of what he had just written about this self-proclaimed champion. "No. I just wrote my father."

The Indian's eyes took on a rather humorous twinkle as he replied, "The horseman is too serious much of the time. I think it would be well if he really did go fishing some time."

The cowboy looked at the Indian and smiled. "Many times I have fished like a fishing fool, my friend . . . In fact, I'll bet you a bottle of our boss' best whiskey what I can out-fish you any day, O' mighty fisherman!"

There was a pause, and then Tecao's voice gained a hitherto unknown resonance as he seemed to gradually transform himself into an impish narrator. "We will fish together some time . . . But Tecao will no longer drink the white man's whiskey while fishing. Strange things have happened to me when I have done this." He had cast out a baited hook, and now waited patiently for a fish to bite.

One did.

"What strange things, for instance?" Troy sat up and turned full attention to this ever-amazing Indian.

Tecao peered back with a poker-faced expression as if having second thoughts about continuing. Finally, he said haltingly, "You won't think me a simple old man . . . Or—tell?"

"No! Certainly not!"

"Well, some years ago I was very fond of fishing, and did much of it in this very stream—but many miles down from where we now sit, where the big fish run in the spring." He paused, playing this fish to the utmost, then continued, "I also took with me the bottled-up lightning. And of course, I would sip it from time to time . . . Anyway, one day I was nipping the fire water and looked down to see a big snake swimming near me. There, captured in his jaws, hung a big bull frog. I like frog legs better than fish, so I reached out and snatched that frog from the snake, and, just as I did, some of the whiskey spilled from the bottle right into that snake's mouth!"

"Imagine that!"

"Yes, . . . Well, I kept the frog in my sack and went on about my fishing, thinking no more of that snake that had swam off without its breakfast." He stopped, looking as though having just played his last card in a losing poker hand.

"Well! Is that all? Some story!" snorted Troy with a dismal display of facial features.

"Not at all . . . After some time I felt something tapping against my leg . . . I looked down, and there . . ." He interrupted himself purposefully.

"What?" Troy interrupted excitedly.

"There—there was that same snake, lookin' right up at me an' with another frog in his mouth!" The old Indian finished and remained cross-legged on the stump, gazing off into the starry vault of sky and was absolutely rigid as a statue.

The young victim suddenly convulsed into uncontrollable laughter. He rolled one way, then the other, howling in fiendish glee at this grand-daddy of all the fish stories he had ever heard, and at his own, unfortunate gullibility.

Finally, his sides ached with the laughter he had not heard nor known for months. Between howls he would look at this Indian, who had hatched up such a joke, but that worthy only sat there grinning as though he had just landed his largest fish—which indeed he had!

Troy's senses finally sobered and he gazed long and keenly at his new friend. The Indian's face had become thoughtful and serious once more, and his obsidian eyes seemed to look through the young rider. When he spoke it came scarcely more than in a whisper. "Young horseman, I will take you with me to the canyon . . . Soon . . . Perhaps it is time." His voice broke slightly and he looked away toward the distant, white cliffs. "One thing is of importance. I wish you to tell no one; not Virginia or anyone else at the ranch. We must pack, unseen and go in the same manner. I fear we will be the cause of much trouble and unnecessary concern if they are made aware of our intent . . . Can you do this?"

"When?"

"Very soon. I will let you know. But you must put your stored supplies together in the next few days. You should do this without attracting attention to yourself and without raising any questions or suspicion."

"I will be ready," Troy replied softly. He gazed momentarily out over the bubbling river, wondering if he had really heard the Indian correctly. It was the word he had been waiting for, and it was true! He turned to Tecao, but the ghost-like Indian was gone as though he had vaporized.

The young rider looked about and listened intently for several moments, then drew himself up and walked the quiet, darkened path toward the ranchero.

CHAPTER 8

TWO RIDERS and their trailing pack horses framed an unexpected and exciting picture to the thin-clad redskin. The young lookout was positioned on a lofty point which jutted above the meandering wash, and just now two strangers were picking their way northward through the brush. The fledgling warrior, looking down from his eagle-like vantage point on the side of Black Rock Peak, was taking his turn from among several other boys in this small tribe. Now his lonely, vigilant days and nights were being rewarded. He snaked slowly away from the rocky rim, and, when he had wormed his way from a possible sighting by the intruders, gained his feet, mounted his pony and began picking his way down the treacherous, northern trail.

IT HAD BEEN logistically simple for Troy to keep secretive his preparations to leave Virginia and the ranchero—the mental situation was another matter. Virginia's recent interest in his every move, coupled with her own obvious admiration for him, continually tugged at his mind. His interest in her had likewise been incensed, and while each tried to act with restraint their natural instincts caused each to realize a desire for closeness of the other. Restraint with apprehension was the mode—Troy in his longing to remain near her, but in the knowledge of his deceitful preparations to do just the opposite, and Virginia in her woman's desire to remain near the young rider without compromising herself, and thus, maintain a slight air of aloofness.

The youngsters had kept each other's company as often as possible since the evening at Tecao's cabin, and Troy's growing desire for the girl caused him quiet grief . . . Now he wondered about her feelings for him. Would she feel contempt for him now? Perhaps she held no respect for him at all—as was the case with Judd Hazelud. At least she would certainly feel deceived and hurt.

"We have been seen," Tecao quietly observed, turning sideways in the saddle to his trailing companion.

Troy bounced rapidly back to the present. "What?" He glanced upward at the dark rocks and lofty crags, now virtually surrounding the break in every direction. "There's no one around for miles."

The Indian poked a thumb over his shoulder. "Black Rock has always been a lookout. I saw no one, but I know someone is or was up there—may already be riding for the cliff or the canyon. Whoever, my people or the Paiute, they will know of our intrusion by this sunset. Perhaps they will not know who we are, friend or otherwise. And it may not matter if they did . . . By the time we reach the old volcano vents or the color cliffs, I think we can expect company."

"Why shouldn't it make a difference who has spotted us?" questioned his young companion. "Your people would certainly recognize you!"

The Indian smirked and replied forcefully, "We will not be asked who we are by long range rifles! We will be welcomed to this area of earth by no man or animal!" He returned to a taciturn state, giving full attention to the terrain ahead and above them.

The riders proceeded quietly. Fully alert to their surroundings, they wove the animals carefully through the scattered and broken volcanic rock. The gray and black cores seemed like tombstones, protruding to form rows as they had been faulted and eventually weathered into view along the deep wash. To the right, huge corduroy rivulets and steps rose to eventually frame white, rising cliffs, and some, millions of years old, were extinct volcanoes of huge size that now formed more sloping and less imposing hills to the left. It was early evening, and the waves of heat seemed to hang in shimmering fashion over the needle grass, causing objects to waver in the distance. Patches and occasional thickets of sage-brush and cholla were but vague objects to be skirted as the riders forced onward.

Troy was rightfully uneasy. He felt the handle of his Colt .45, lifted the weapon repeatedly and dropped it into the holster, finally making certain that it was secure but readily available. Looking high into the darkening cliffs he suddenly wished he had been able to stake himself to a rifle. He and the Indian were both good shots with the six-shooters, they had proved it to each other. But, in this terrain, revolvers would be little match for a Sharps, or a Henry like Jim O'Neill had possessed. And they would be even less valuable against a rifle such as the new Winchester that John Grayson had recently purchased.

The young rider could dance a can or bore larger targets quickly and accurately up to 30 yards, but beyond that the accuracy of aim along with the velocity of pistol bullets each fell off drastically. If anyone were to lie in ambush up in those rocks, and possessed a rifle . . . .

The hours passed painfully slow as the sun continued on its course, eventually to tip the western peaks with crimson. The rocky, meandering stream turned to a mere rivulet, and the yawning valley to but a narrow slit between the high faults. Ahead through the buttresses loomed pale pink and gray cliffs.

Skipping streaks suddenly frothed the sand around the riders, and out of the gray ahead burst specks of red flame. Rifles cracked, echoed repeatedly, and cracked again. The men emptied their saddles and scrambled for protection among the rocks as their mounts and pack horses scattered and milled around.

Troy pulled his .45 and glanced sideways for a sign from Tecao, now crouched behind a boulder to his right. The Indian was already triggering at what Troy could also see—slithering and gliding shadows that moved slowly but relentlessly toward them along both sides of the break.

Occasional red spurts flashed through the air as an enemy halted and fired from a protective position. Most of the lead thudded harmlessly around them in the rocks and large boulders, but one suddenly spat sand into Troy's face, momentarily blinding him. It had been fired from a close position to his left and above, and he rolled aside to flatten himself into a depression in the ground, rubbing the grinding sand from his face. Through stinging vision he attempted to catch a glimpse of this bold adversary who had gained such a threatening position. He carefully raised the six-gun and triggered it toward a moving shadow amid the rocks, and a yelp went up as an Indian raised slightly, took a step forward and then faded into the ground. There was a momentary ease in the gunfire and Troy stole a glance at Tecao.

"Pauite," the Indian stated. "Not many. Five or six. Like to know where they got those guns!" Then he forced a grim smile. "According to another, more useless legend, they're supposed to be using tomahawks and arrows—Keep your white head down!"

Troy found little humor in the situation and grimly addressed all his faculties toward the advancing menace . . . It was nearly dark, and he had heard somewhere that Paiute Indians normally didn't attack at night. If Tecao had judged correctly and these were Paiute, then they would soon melt into the darkness and await morning's first light to resume their assault. But if the wise old man was mistaken, and perhaps these were renegade remnants of the Aztecan band, then an attack of any sort at any time was imminent. It surely remained a matter of moments before the savages grew bolder and would make their inevitable, whooping rush to close quarters, where they would shoot, tomahawk, and undoubtedly scalp the intruders in a horrible blood bath of appalling shrieks and war-cries . . .

The rolls and echoes and gunfire diminished almost as rapidly as they had begun. Troy breathed deeply as he tried to regain the lost confidence. It seemed they had repulsed this initial assault. But it was dark now and he no longer could see his companion. Listening intently, he heard the Indian stir slightly, one of his Colts rubbing against stone as he made a rapid movement. Any noise at all was unlike the Indian, but it was followed by a total silence that dispelled the young rider's fear.

Then, after a long continued silence, Troy strained in an attempt to hear any motion or sound ahead or around him. The only evidence of life suddenly came by way of a low whinny. It was Sundown, and the frightened animal could be heard picking his way through the rocks below and down the back trail. Troy turned toward the Indian's position.

"Tecao?" His voice echoed lightly off the slope and there came no reply. The young rider retreated behind the boulder's protection, intense fear overcoming him. Tecao was not there. The thoughts spun through his brain. Surely his partner had been taken captive! No, he could lay dead or dying mere feet away. Maybe he had run off! . . . No! Slowly he calmed, and when again secure within, crept slowly in the direction of the Indian's last position. Locating the boulder, his groping hands came up with several spent cartridges—but the Indian was gone. He leaned heavily against the missile as he pondered the situation.

If the Paiute had captured Tecao, it was certainty they would return for Troy at first light. There would be no safety here. He must make some sort of move. Even now the Paiute could be circling his position . . . He would get to Sundown and make an attempt at locating one of the pack animals, and the sooner the better!

There was a scuffling of hoofs that grew louder until he was certain there was a rider or at least a horse moving along the up-trail. Then suddenly the old Indian walked upon him in the hazy moonlight, all four animals in tow.

"Tecao! Thank God it's you! I thought . . ."

The Indian walked up to Troy and peered directly into the ghost-like face. "You thought I had been captured, or—or that I had perhaps run away," he said calmly. "My young rider, you have much to learn about this old one before our ride is finished . . . It was necessary to regain the horses, which I did as soon as I could safely move. By morning they would have been well on their way to the ranch. And we—well, we would make a tragic sight, trying to move on lacking supplies or a quick way to travel. The horses would have also created much undue alarm for those at the ranchero . . . We will not remain here for sunrise. I can follow the trail and we will go on at once. We'll be at the canyon before the sun sets tomorrow." There was a long pause and then he said thoughtfully, "If you feel a bit foolish, young rider, then that is because you should. Remember that nobody can make a fool out of you—you do that to yourself!"

Thus chastised, Troy also felt momentarily placated by the darkness as he fought to hold in a tear of joy, and a warmth swept through his body. The Indian seemed absolutely infallible, and never again would he doubt the loyalty or ability of this new friend . . . They mounted and moved quietly through the ever-narrowing passage.

CHAPTER 9

JUDD HAZELUD nursed much more than a cracked gun hand and the several superficial cuts and bruises that had been inflicted upon the remainder of his person. Doc Hathaway, one of the few non-quacks in Kanab, had accomplished a superlative job in cleaning and stitching up the wounds. But he recognized a wound in Judd that he could never heal, and in a small way attempted to inform the ungrateful patient. Seeing that this was an act of futility, he finally informed Judd with a knowing look that he had best begin practicing whatever trade he intended to pursue with the left wing.

Thus Hazelud's next order of business was to procure a holster for the left side. Then he rented a room over the Hay Burner where he spent several weeks, not only recouping from his physical wounds but coaxing his left hand to draw and aim accurately.

The days of pacing the matchboard floor also gave him time in which to think about his situation. The feeling of hate, arising from his fateful encounter at the ranchero, was but a faint memory compared to his present state of mind. He seethed inside.

In the beginning, there had been the matter of gaining the hand of Virginia, along with the eventual control of the Ranchero Johnson. Now remained only a lust for revenge—a revenge now so spiteful that he would henceforth gladly take on anyone and everyone who may stand in the way of his drive to even the score.

Gradually, as the hand and shoulder improved, along with the wretched man's expertise at southpaw gun handling, an idea framed itself in his sickened mind.

O'Neill either was now, or was destined to be, heading for the canyon and toward the treasure that just could be a reality. That treasure, if any, could and would be Judd's. Virginia had professed what had obviously been her lingering hate for him, but she too could yet be his. And he might use her as the bait to get at O'Neill! Yes, he thought, he would kill Troy, he would have the girl, and he would indeed secure whatever treasure there might be for himself.

On that afternoon Hazelud visited the Gold Digger's Supply Store, to return with an oil skin bundle, which he carefully placed beneath saddle blankets in a corner of his room. A grim smile overcame him as he marveled at his own, ingenious plan.

TWO DAYS had passed since the Graysons' discovery that Troy and Tecao had left the ranchero. It had been expected and thus an unalarming event to both John and Martha Grayson, since they had considered it merely a matter of time before these new and mutually trusting friends went on their inevitable quest. Grayson had seen the two in company often and watched their admiration for one another grow; Troy becoming increasingly attached to the Indian and Tecao's growing, protective instincts over the young rider. The rancher was neither surprised nor disappointed.

Virginia was not really surprised at their departure, but her mind quarreled with their manner of leaving. She had romanticized a scene of repeated requests and pleadings by her young lover—for he was indeed that now—and of an incessant barrage of love returned by her; love that would keep him within her grasp, perhaps for always.

One thought common to all was that Tecao had been the wise thinker, for it was he who would have planned the maneuver; he who would have recognized what further procrastination would do to Troy's plan. And he had craftily averted any such circumstance.

Virginia turned over these facts as she rode the up-canyon trail toward the old cabin under the wall. This visit to the Indian's quarters would bring no positive relief to her situation, but it would bring her closer to Troy in memory. She missed him and loved him, and the memory of their meeting with the Indian at this place would forever remain in her heart.

The noon-day sun blazed down on the empty lean-to, and a wisp of wind curled tiny sand devils around the open door and stirred the sand along the canyon wall. She had a sudden, strange sensation of someone else's presence and started to wheel her mount around. But at this moment Judd Hazelud took several long strides around the corner of the cabin and firmly grasped her horse's bridle.

Virginia sputtered as she cuffed his arm in a vain attempt to force his release . . . "Judd! What—what on earth are you doing? . . . Let me go!"

The outlaw grinned wickedly upward as he matched the horse's side steps, pulling until he had the animal under control. "Doin'?" he echoed, acting as a cat might with a mouse. "Doin? Shore y'u can see what I'm a'doin'! I've watched y'u for days—followed y'u—an I got y'u now!" His voice was powerful and totally feelingless for the youngster.

Virginia needed to hear no more to wholly recognize her peril, and at this she whitened visibly. "Judd Hazelud, if you harm me my daddy will kill you! Or—or . . ."

"Or yore Mister O'Neill?" mocked her captor, and he spit vehemently under her mount. "Wal, yo'r savior is a two-day ride from heah!" Then his face brightened with a wicked thought. "Y'u can see him soon though, at thet. An' he'll certainly enjoy it, I'm shore. Now, git down off'n thet hoss!" He reached out and not kindly tugged her from the stirrups.

Virginia found tears as she stood helplessly in Judd's rough grasp. "What are you intending to do with me?" she questioned, as a barrage of frightening situations flashed to mind. Then she looked at him with the full realization that at this moment he was a desperate man who was quite capable of anything. She was wholly frightened for her life, and Hazelud showed that he knew it. "You're kidnapping me!"

"Very good for openers," mused Hazelud, drunk with the power he possessed over her, and he kept a firm grip on her arm. "An' if'n y'u play yo'r cards the way yo'r told ta, y'u may even stay alive. Y'u and I are goin' on a long ride, Ginny Grayson. I'd advise y'u not to try a get-away either, as thet won't go easy on that pretty face of your'n." His eyes roamed over her full length with some interest, then continued factually, "At least yo'r dressed for where we're goin'!"

His look and tone made Virginia at least grateful she had worn riding clothes for this occasion. She was confused, but knew she must think clearly. She had to find a way to escape, as this fool actually intended to force her accompaniment into the mountains! Then it flashed clearly to her. Hazelud wanted her, but he was going to find Troy and use her as a pawn to kill him. And he would end up killing her, too. The treasure! Yes, he would be after that too. This was his basic animal plan. She pulled her shoulder from Judd's grip with a sudden movement and vaulted for her saddle. Rough hands reached out and hauled her from it once more, and she fell to the ground, looking up to see and feel those same hands strike soundly to either side of her face. She leaned backward on her elbows, dazed by the blows.

When she regained her senses, Virginia was flopped forward astride her horse with both hands secured to the pommel of the saddle. She was jostled roughly from side to side as the animal trotted over the pocked terrain. Early evening was fading, but she could discern Hazelud ahead on his mount, and a pack horse was tied between them.

Gradually, she cleared the cobwebs from her mind until she could think clearly . . . Physically she was no match for the massive Judd, and he now held control over her total situation—this was not likely to be easily overcome. She would be at his mercy except for her own wits, and Judd would be no match for her on an equal, thinking basis. She must try to outsmart him. If she failed, then Troy surely would become this animal's victim. And she—well, she may be in for a fate worse than a sudden death. She shuddered at her own, morbid thoughts . . . Perhaps if she were to play along with Judd's plan—pretend to commit herself to the inevitable—perhaps then she would be in a position to warn Troy, and at least save his life . . . Her life may become another matter.

IT REMINDED HIM SOMEWHAT OF A HUGE CHESSBOARD STREWN WITH CHESSMEN — ALL RAVAGED BY THE BATTLE OF TIME.

CHAPTER 10

AS EVENING APPROACHED, the riders halted to discuss the terrain they now faced. Tecao at first argued that a trail leading into the canyon from the north end would be safer for the descent, but his lack of persistence and Troy's firm stand upon the use of his uncle's map won out. Thus they approached the abyss from a south-westerly direction.

The Indian cautioned against broaching the rim, where any movement would become silhouetted by the setting sun and easily spotted from below. So they maintained a distance from the whistling, wind-swept cliffs and carefully navigated the rugged hills and ridges along-side.

The key point on Troy's map would be the small creek, or perhaps its dried bed, which Jim O'Neill had proclaimed had led him down an obscure path along the wall. They had passed beyond a small rent that was strewn with small rocks when the Indian suddenly reined up. One arm upward in a show of caution, he listened intently a moment and then gestured toward the canyon with his head. "Hear?"

"Nary a thing," replied Troy, cupping his hand and bending an ear in the direction indicated by Tecao. Then the faint sound of trickling water touched his ear. "Yes! There's water over here somewhere!" He spurred toward a small cut, closer to the rim, and suddenly he gazed down upon a small creek that cascaded a snake-like path downward and through a narrow, winding gorge. "This has to be it. He said it was next to impossible to find, and we rode right over it without knowing it was there!"

The Indian's reply lacked his young companion's enthusiasm. "We will make camp here for the night and take the trail down tomorrow."

The two consumed a fireless meal consisting of dried beef and biscuits, and during this the youngster paused often to look upon the canyon. It was exactly as his uncle had proclaimed; a giant arena filled with towering, sandstone statues and wind-sculptured figures. It reminded him somewhat of a huge chessboard strewn with chessmen, some seemingly alive and ready to do battle—others staunch and conservative looking—but all ravaged by the big battle with time. He recalled with a sudden chill that one of these players would be a queen-like figure, located somewhere near the treasure, but his eyes searched vainly for such a prominence among the giants.

The Indian interrupted the quiet evening as he looked over his nose at the youngster. "So, what is this thing that you have read so much about?"

"Archaeology. It's a manner of studying what we call artifacts—items that were used or owned by people long ago. From these we're sometimes able to put together bits and pieces of information which may form a pattern of history of how they lived, thought, survived, or perhaps, died." He eyed his listener expectantly, and the Indian nodded in a go-ahead gesture.

"There is much of interest to the archaeologist in this very spot. Perhaps of most interest is the real history of the Indians themselves. I've read that many tribes and bands inhabited this area for hundreds of years—perhaps thousands—before any white men came here. Most were part of the Southern Paiute, whose ancestry perhaps dates way into ancient history . . . To now my studies have been nearly all from university books my mother procured out east, but one day there will certainly be a university in the Southwest, where there would be easy access to these artifacts. I would like to be a part of such a university, and to study this area more thoroughly."

The Indian was momentarily thoughtful, as though perhaps contemplating this infringement upon his ancestry. Finally, he inquired, "This study you do—these articles you hope to find—perhaps they will be of great value in money to you?"

"That's possible. All manner of priceless items have been unearthed by archaeologists—professionals and amateurs alike . . . In the country of Egypt they have unearthed old tombs and chambers that were literally filled with items of gold, and precious stones. There are reports of other such finds throughout the world—several are nearby, down in Mexico."

Tecao questioned rapidly, "You have studied of the great one of Mexico, Montezuma?"

Troy showed his amazement, then replied, "Yes, I've read much about the Aztec nation led by Montezuma and his great father before him. That nation prospered in Central America for nearly 2,000 years."

"Then you know that the white men came and destroyed that civilization!" Tecao rang out in a vitreous tone.

Troy was quiet on the moment and merely looked at the Indian, who now was reclined, staring off into the mile-high sky. After careful deliberation, he said, "Yes, I know. A Spaniard, Cortez, deceived the great warrior and his nation in order to gain favor and riches for himself and the king of Spain. Cortez was a man of greed, and searched constantly for treasure, as was the pattern of the so-called Conquistadors. He was . . ."

"He was a fool!" Tecao poignantly interrupted. "He and many other white men have plundered our land for wealth . . . My people told much of another Spaniard—one they called Coronado . . . Have you also read of that one?"

"I've read several accounts concerning the exploits of Francisco Coronado. He explored much of your territory a little over 300 years ago. And you were right. His quest was also for gold. He searched many years for the fabled seven cities of Cibola, said to be built almost entirely of gold, and first reported by another Spaniard named Marcos de Niza . . . But Coronado was the first white man to look upon the Grand Canyon, and in 1540 he also came close to this very area, if in fact he was not here. In all of his travels he found little wealth to speak of, but he did much to explore the territory . . . One thing seems certain, he knew little and perhaps cared less for the history of the people upon whose land he trespassed. By archaeological standards, he was certainly a poor scientist!"

The Indian shifted his gaze from the vault of sky to his young companion again. Then he half asked, half stated, "It seems that you are one who is more concerned with becoming a seeker of history than one who looks merely for gold and other treasures." He paused and then stated factually, "In the morning we will find our way down to the canyon floor."

Troy sat a long time in silence, reflecting the recent happenings. He was sent into a quandary of thoughts, and he knew that something was just not right. There were too many questions concerning this Indian, and he suddenly

realized that he could not put a handle on any of them . . .
He recollected the night that he and Virginia had visited
the lean-to, and the bird-like design that Tecao had absently
drawn in the sand. Obviously the Indian knew that sign well,
and hadn't he stated that he had lived in this canyon as a
boy? Then this also made the chance exceptionally good that
the worthy also knew of this trace into the canyon. In fact, he
probably had been in or out by this path before now. And,
had he not been quick to point out the trace, which they had
actually ridden over and beyond?

"Tecao?"

There was silence, but he could see the Indian's stone-like,
chiseled face outlined in the moonlight. The Indian either
slept or preferred not to hear.

Troy was aroused. He would question Tecao further, and
now. Often he had wondered at the approach he might make
concerning the bird sign. Now was the time, and he was not
going to be denied this moment of inner strength. He rose
suddenly to a commanding posture beside his partner and
repeated his inquiry, "Tecao?"

The Indian stirred and flashed angrily, "I am here! What
is it you ask?"

Troy shrank under a hesitant thought of his own
boldness, then looked again at his prone companion, took a
breath and questioned, "We're friends, are we not?"

The Indian's tone was less vitreous, "Yes."

"You have made many statements about this canyon, and
but a few concerning yourself. And—and you haven't told
me all there is to know. I'm certain of it."

The old man rose slowly to his haunches, where he
balanced and peered back at his young friend. "I'm sure I
don't know everything," he stated, with a hint of poignancy
returning.

Troy withered momentarily upon the fringe of retreat, then, regaining courage, he stated matter-of-factly, "I believe that you know much more than we have discussed in friendship. I also think you know this trail into the canyon—perhaps know it well. If you lived here once, as you've said, then you would know the canyon and its people quite well. I saw you draw the triangular bird sign in the sand by your cabin that night Virginia and I were there." He paused and then continued passionately, "You were also nearby when Judd nearly killed Virginia and me! I also know you would have killed Hazelud if Grayson hadn't interfered when he did . . . You have since become my best friend, and certainly my protector. And still—still you are hiding something from me. I can feel it!"

The Indian spun slightly aside as he rose slowly to his full height. In this manner he stood in the moonlight, hands now stretched overhead and his back to the young rider. Then he turned slowly, he being the one who had now assumed the commanding position, towering by half a foot over the other. Then his left hand moved to clutch within his buckskin shirt, and he withdrew it suddenly. The extended hand came to halt mere inches from Troy's face.

The young man saw the object clearly. It swung as a pendulum might, was secured to a rawhide thong, and several jewels sparkled from it as raindrops might from a swaying twig. The bright, metallic object was slightly twisted and easily recognized by Jim O'Neill's description of it. It was the segment of bracelet! Awed, Troy shrank back several paces.

The Indian well recognized this impression upon the young rider. He quickly relaxed, took a step forward and placed the link of bracelet in Troy's hand. "Take it. It belongs to you, young rider, just as it belonged to your uncle . . . Let us sit upon the stones . . . There is something I will say now."

Troy O'Neill accepted the bracelet and sank upon a boulder, bewildered inwardly and totally unable to cement his thoughts.

Tecao crouched nearby and looked off into the darkness that now totally engulfed the canyon. He spoke slowly and deliberately to the young man. "I have wanted to explain certain things to you, and many times. It has never seemed to be the right time to do so—surely it is not now, I have preferred to wait—to lead you to your treasure first . . . For your uncle did not lie to you. There is a treasure—a very ancient one by your terms—and it exists much as in the story that has been told for many years. Your uncle was close upon it, just as he told you, and he returned for it recently, as you suspected he did . . . That night at the ranchero I showed you and Virginia my Paiute arrow wound. If you had looked closer you would have seen it was a pistol shot, not an arrow, that did the damage. That pistol was held by your uncle, and it nearly killed me." He stopped and emitted a brief sigh of reluctance. "You will not find him alive in this canyon, or anywhere else for that matter. He is dead. He nearly killed me, but it is he who now lies buried.

Troy felt a flurry of feelings. There were no words to say, and he merely stared at the Indian.

Tecao's voice lost its poignancy and he continued quietly, "Your uncle Jim was no doubt a good man, but he was possessed with man's greatest enemy—the lust for wealth. I am indeed sorry for him and you, young rider, for I knew neither of you at the time. He is dead at these hands, and by my knife. And you—well, you I have come to know and to think of as a son I did not have.

"This canyon is mine, just as it had belonged to and been protected by my people for many generations. I did not lie to you about my Aztecan birthright, nor about my people, who are scarce in numbers now. I am perhaps the final strong one among my tribe, and soon, I think, the sun will likewise set over my own grave . . .

"I left this canyon many years ago. I did so at first to live with, and learn about, those who would be our enemies. I had hoped to seek truth and perhaps some manner by which to prolong what would one day certainly be, and perhaps is now, a reality at hand—the end of my people, and, the end of our cause."

There was a lengthy, ominous pause, during which neither man spoke out. When one did, it was the Indian once more. "The Aztecan people have ranged many miles in all directions from where we now sit. The tribe was here in fact many years prior to the coming of my small group of Aztec ancestors—they are known to you as the Uto-Aztecan people. Three hundred years ago, when Cortez ravaged my people in old Mexico, Emperor Montezuma sent out a secret caravan. It left just before he was killed. The caravan carried much gold, silver and many jewels and artifacts—as you call them—it was much of the wealth of the Aztec nation. My father told me the story many times. He said that instructions had been given the officers in charge—one of these being Montezuma's nephew—to hide the treasure where it would never be found and then to make certain that none of the warriors who made up the caravan lived to tell the secret."

"That's incredible! You mean they were told to kill them all, and then each other?" Troy asked, returning the intensity of the moment.

"Yes. And when the treasure was hidden, they proceeded to kill the other warriors as instructed. And, when just the two remained, they fought to the death."

"I AM A DIRECT DECENDANT OF MONTEZUMA, AND I CARRY HIS NAME."

Montezuma's nephew won over the other. But when this happened and he had placed the other warrior's head in a symbolic manner to protect the cache, he had a decision to make about himself . . . He must either take his own life or live out his remaining days at the very spot, protecting the treasure from anyone who may have chanced to witness what had taken place in the canyon."

"That explains the 17 skulls that Uncle Jim found. Then Montezuma's nephew actually lived. But—but, he must have taken a wife and had children . . ." Troy broke off, amazed.

"His name was Iuicamin. And yes, he found a woman eventually, from among the Utes . . . I, Tecao, am one of their direct descendants."

"But, you left them, and the canyon?"

"Yes, I left the first time when very young. I lived with a white man and woman—kind, backwoods people who had built a home in the mountains west of here. They had four children of their own, but cared about what happened to me and taught me the white man's tongue. I lived with them seven years, and cried when they and three of their own children were killed by a party of Paiute warriors. Their surviving son, Steven, ran into the distant hills. I searched endlessly for him, but I fear he too was lost."

The two men eyed one another at length, then the Indian arose, took several paces toward the rim of the canyon, and stated simply, "I am a direct descendant of Emperor Montezuma, and I carry his name."

"Your given name, then is Tecao Montezuma!"

"Yes, I am Montezuma." The old warrior still stood with his back to Troy and facing eastward. "And I am now the last of my people, I fear."

Troy tried to let this entire development sink into his brain. Finally, he inquired, "Why have you agreed to lead me to the treasure, since you are its protector?"

The Indian remained facing away as he replied, "Many reasons. I have just told you that I may have no followers to carry on with its protection. Surely if not guarded it will eventually be ravaged by the Paiute—or worse, by greedy white men . . . More importantly, I have told you all this because I believe your interest to be more in its history and significance to my people than its value in wealth to you. Also, you study the white man's religion, and I think you to be a good man inside."

Then the Indian turned toward the young rider, with his face now sternly outlined in the vaulted night. "You must make me one promise."

"What is your request?" the youngster slowly breathed.

"That you will show no person of greed its location, and that you will use any riches you gain to build this great university of learning you have spoken of . . . And, there is one last thing. You must do all within your power to unite the feelings of white men and their Indian brothers. There is much likeness between them, and they must seek to understand one another."

Tecao halted a moment, then said with deep feeling, "Perhaps such understanding can come from the teachings within your book of good things, as well as the thing you call archaeology. Whichever you choose to follow, do you promise to do what is right?"

"Yes," was the only, but solemn reply.

The Indian abruptly went back to his pack, and with no further talk proceeded to unroll his blanket. Then he fell heavily and clutched it about him. Again the aging warrior had terminated an amazing interview with the young rider from Arizona.

Troy rolled a blanked about himself and likewise settled down. But the sleepless hours dragged on, and there were still too many questions on his mind, as well as new answers that must now be digested.

It seemed almost unreal, as in a dream. He played the heavy segment of bracelet about in his hand . . . It was certainly real, and there would be no sleep for Troy O'Neill on this night.

CHAPTER 11

THE HAVOC WROUGHT upon the beautiful, young lady of the ranchero by the implacable Judd Hazelud was indeed taking its toll. There had been no let up in their steady trek from noon until night fall, and Virginia was the recipient of much pain. Accustomed as she had always been to a saddle, this ride, with her hands bound by leather to the saddle horn, rendered her totally unable to adjust to the movements of her mount. The pain in her back and legs grew worse as the day wore thin, and she repeatedly trifled on the edge of fainting. She felt a total outrage, but upon the several times she had wretchedly denounced her captor, had been met only with an icy stare.

Hazelud had been otherwise noncommittal. He rode always in the fore, glancing back at his captive only so often as to reassure himself that she and the pack animal were in tow.

Virginia knew part of the terrain, and she also recognized when they had passed beyond the area which held any familiarity. She also saw what Judd was following—the clear trail left by horses and riders that had but recently passed this way. She knew these had to be left by Troy and Tecao, and that tracks of any sort would be likely to remain many days at this arid time of year.

The sun was disappearing over the western ridge, and an evening chill was rapidly settling in as Hazelud halted the small procession. He guessed correctly that his captive would not, and probably could not, attempt an escape at this time, so he untied her hands roughly and left her to dismount when and however she could.

Not uttering a word, Hazelud set about preparing a makeshift camp. He would not risk a fire, but unpacked dried beef jerky and bread, making no comment nor move as Virginia chose to seek private refuge around a small bend in the stream.

Virginia, sore and dirty with trail dust from head to toe, let the cool water return some of the feeling to her hands. When her moment of refuge was complete, she returned to Judd's view and ate sparingly of the items he had lain on a blanket. Then she made rapid her preparations for the night, taking the bed roll Judd had tossed to the ground near her, and once more searching out some privacy. She would sleep as far from him as possible, but, realizing that her captor sat devouring her every move, she settled upon a spot between two boulders which was not far from the horses and within Hazelud's view. Fully clothed, she settled for the night.

Virginia was filled with exhaustion, but she was likewise filled with a few thoughts of what her captor may attempt to do to her. So she tossed at lengths, trying to cement ideas or a plan. She and Judd would both be conscious of one fact—by this time her father would have discovered her plight at the hands of his late foreman, or at least would have concluded by now that she would have run off with, or attempted to follow, Troy and the Indian. The latter would not be too difficult to weed out, as there would be no evidence of preparedness by her for such a long and arduous ride. In any event, Virginia felt a resurgence of spirit by the fact that at this very moment her father and most of the ranch hands were pounding the trail northward to her rescue. She rolled to the side and stole a quick glance at Judd Hazelud. He had built a cigarette, and now rapped its firefly-like light protectively in one hand as he sat, idly looking over the area. The culprit neither looked at her nor showed the slightest interest toward her on this moment. She relaxed and gradually drifted into a dreamy, light state of sleep . . . .

THE ONLY TRAINS Virginia had ever seen were those belching flame and smoke within the pages of magazines or books. Now she had the sudden feeling that she must be on one. Yes, she now recognized the interior of the last car on such trains—she was inside a caboose! Her hands and feet were tightly bound, and she was being jostled from side to side as the noisy, swinging beast lurched along as on a runaway track.

Virginia's eyes pried the cold haze that surrounded her everywhere, and finally she spied Judd Hazelud. That worthy was at the other end of the car, and was perched high atop a large pile of gleaming, golden artifacts. He leered at her, laughing boisterously, while occasionally pausing to puff heavily on an immense cigar.

The train was gaining momentum and it yawed and pitched in flight. Virginia tried to scream, but no sound came from her open lips. She saw Hazelud again. He held a gun and it was poised upward toward the narrow doorway over her head. Her senses told her that at any moment a figure would burst through that door and into the caboose . . . In her dream's eye she could see her lover cautiously working his way along the platform toward that door. Surely he would momentarily spring inside, only to face point-blank lead from Hazelud's six-gun. Troy O'Neill did just that, and just as Virginia lurched desperately to her feet. The roar of

Judd's weapon filled the small caboose, and the young lady of the Ranchero Johnson fell dead at the feet of her lover . . .

"Git up! We're movin' on! Cain't wait whilst we're bein' follered!"

Virginia bolted to a sitting position, at first uncertain of her whereabouts. Hazelud had bent over her, and he drew up quickly at her frightful expression.

Virginia ferreted out fact from dream. It was not even close to dawn, and her captor, certain she was now fully awake, turned to repacking the horses. His hurried movements told Virginia that he had no intention of preparing food, and she was hungry . . . With thoughts still jumbled from her perplexing situation, she thought about the need to escape or to gain control over Judd. Perhaps a way could be found to stall or otherwise impede their rapid progress. She premeditated. Her father had said that it was a mere two or three day ride to the big canyon, and at this accelerated rate she became certain that no posse or rider could catch them before reaching it. She must do something. Perhaps she could leave some sort of trail by dropping items of her own along the way, providing Judd did not bind her hands once more. No, this would be a worthless gesture, as the trail they now left could be followed by almost a blind man. The best approach may come from conversation itself, which thus far her captor had shown a reluctance to do. It was at least an idea, so she decided to approach him. This she did as he was attending the horses.

"Aren't we having anything to eat?" Virginia spoke in a soft, servile manner.

Judd was obviously rattled at her abnormal approach, but nevertheless he fumbled about in a pack and drew forth a packet of dried beef, handed it to her without a word and turned once more to the pack horse. Then he hesitated, turning his head toward her, and stated flatly, "No time for eats, really. Y'u know we're bein' follered."

"Well, I'm starved, so thank you, Judd." Then, as if an after-though, she added, "You won't tie my hands this time, will you, Judd? It really isn't necessary, you know."

"No. Y'u ain't goin' nowhere up ahead. No need." He half gestured at their surroundings, which were indeed wild and bleak.

Virginia moved a step closer to her target, chewing on the beef and feigning an air of carelessness. "What do you intend doing with me, Judd?"

He turned to look at her incredulously, his voice taking on an unnerved tone, and without the evil grin or vengeful look on his face. He stared through the dim light at this beautiful girl he had once hoped to claim as his own.

"Do with y'u? I already told y'u—y'u know what Troy and that Injin' are after in that canyon. Gold, or some treasure . . . Mor'n a man can handle, I reckon. An' it must be there, or that Injin never would'v taken him there! Well," he half stuttered, "I aim ta git that gold fer me, and—an fer y'u too, if'n y'u come along peaceable."

"But you said you wanted to kill Troy!" she stated enigmatically.

"Won't really kill nobody—not less'n I have ta . . . Kilt a fella once't—had ta—will again, if'n I have ta," he stated repetitively. Then a hint of warning permeated his voice. "I'd be careful. Y'u been askin' too many questions!"

Judd turned with that and strolled to his saddle, which he lifted and then quickly dropped aside to retrieve an oilskin package. His sudden concern made it obvious to Virginia that he had momentarily forgotten its presence. Then, having snatched it up, he half hid the parcel as he moved to stuff it securely into one of his saddlebags.

Virginia eyed his actions with wonderment, but decided against questioning him upon the moment. Further interrogation now could only serve to rile Hazelud once more. However, she would try to discover the contents of the oilskin at the earliest opportunity. It perhaps was meant to play an important roll in Judd's plans . . . She turned, quickly saddled her mount and stepped up, awaiting Judd's confounded look and his order to move onward in the shivering dawn.

CHAPTER 12

IN MANY PLACES the trail downward was almost nonexistent, while it was narrow and treacherous at each and every step. Riding was impossible, so they proceeded on foot, leading the horses. The Indian went first and they progressed in a somewhat sliding manner, almost totally out of control at some points.

The narrow path crisscrossed the tiny, cascading creek bed, and at times all but disappeared in tangles of vegetation. By mid-morning they had reached a point where the stream had totally disappeared underground, and at this place other rocky cliffs joined their own path in triangular fashion. It was as if they had reached three forks in a road.

Troy recalled the map and his uncle's description of the trace. 'At a place where three escarpments come together you will find a bird-like triangular figure carved in a rock. It points toward the correct fault downward.'

"Wait." The Indian halted at Troy's command, and stood patiently beside his horse as the young cowboy poked high and low along the many facets of rocky projections and tangled vegetation that climbed the ridges. Finally he began edging upward along the southernmost wall. Suddenly he was looking at it—unchanged by the winds and weather of time—the sign that he was certain would be there. It was unnecessary to summon the old Indian, as he quickly appeared at Troy's side. The men ran their fingers along the ancient triangle, which pointed in its flight toward the left fork of the escarpment. It appeared as if chiseled out by metal or sharp stone, and had at one time been openly and prominently displayed on this flat spot along the vertical wall.

"Yes. It is the mark," Tecao said enthusiastically. "It and the others have been placed amid the canyon and its walls for over three hundred years. I have known of the sign, as well as of this trail into the canyon for many years. But I have not looked upon this particular sign until now . . . There are also many like it in the caves below."

"It is just as my uncle said, and see, it points down the left fork, just as he said it did!"

The Indian commented no further, but instead moved carefully down the cliff with the wary, lathered horses.

Jim O'Neill's account again proved true, as this part of the downward trail became nearly impossible to descend. It took several hours of careful, hand-to-brush action to make it down. The horses slid much of the way, and on one occasion a pack animal completely lost its footing. The Indian tugged as it rolled over several times and miraculously came up on all fours, snorting heavily but physically uninjured. Finally, as also prescribed, this trail culminated in the abrupt appearance of a fault which was an evident, dead end.

This, then would be the place where they should search for a narrow, nearly obscured passageway which would descend to the canyon floor itself. But search as he would, no such passage became visible to Troy.

Finally the young rider turned to the Indian, a look of desperation framing his face. "You said you were familiar with this trail. If so, then you should know where the pass is."

THEY STOOD AT THE MOUTH OF A HUGE CAVE, WHICH LOOKED FROM SEVERAL HUNDRED FEET ABOVE THE CANYON FLOOR.

Tecao had once again merely stood beside his horse and watched patiently as the young worthy had poked among the crevices and corners in haste. "You look in the wrong places, it seems." He took a step forward and pointed ahead with a crooked finger. "It is right here, straight ahead."

Troy gazed again. There was nothing ahead but a precipice which fell straight forward into the depths of the canyon below.

Scattered about the face of the bluff were many boulders that were fringed by scarce growths of pinions and mesquite. Tecao headed straight for one of the larger stones, saying simply, "Follow." Troy did, and again the Indian was not wrong. To the left of the boulder a narrow crevice angled downward, almost splitting the heart of the cliff.

They took this descent with utmost care, and found it to be truly a jungle-like, subterranean passageway. It was nearly too small for the horses, underground and dark a good deal of the way. Treacherous stones pocked the trail and rattled downward as men and horses loosened them. The animals snorted in fear and scrambled wildly to keep from cascading headlong in uncontrolled fall. Troy was praying for a more generous passageway when the trail suddenly bottomed out, widening to a degree.

Through the echoing walls of darkness they now made their way toward a faint ray of distant light. The young rider's heart pumped uncontrolled as he fought desire to halt and rest, and then he proceeded onward, the sweat soaking his clothing. This was it! Here was the cave that Jim O'Neill said he had located years ago, and here also was the excitement and adventure that it promised.

Tecao halted as the cave widened and became bright with the light of outdoors. Troy moved alongside his partner, dropping the reins of Sundown and the longer rope attached to the pack horse as he went. Then they stood at the mouth of a huge cave, which looked out from several hundred feet above the canyon floor. It commanded a tremendous view of the entire southern end of the canyon, and rather than looking down at the huge sandstone spires, the prominences now rose before and towered above them. They still appeared stately and figurine-like, with their red, purple and various hues blending as from an artist's easel. But now one could see their roughness and grotesque, wind-carved edges.

"By all that's holy!" exclaimed Troy. "This is absolutely unbelievable!"

"It is that," stated the Indian matter-of-factly. "And, my young Arizona rider, you are looking at the home of my ancestors, bleak as it is."

"How in the world could people survive down here?" queried Troy. "It's drier than a lime kiln, not many trees, an—"

"Huh," Tecao grunted. "I told you that we lived here, not that it was a picnic! . . . That is one reason why I must look for my people—to see if any still live. As for water, it is not plentiful, but the underground stream exists throughout the seasons, as you can see." He indicated toward his left where the horses now nosed one another in and out of a small trickling pocket of water.

Whereupon the men each satisfied their own thirst. Then they filled all the canteens and set about unpacking the horses and making camp. The sun stood straight over the canyon as the housekeeping chores were complete, the horses cared for, and a goodly sum of meat and bread had been consumed.

The young adventurer moved carefully about the cavern, surveying the petroglyphs that seemed to be everywhere on its walls. Some of these he sketched carefully in a notebook.

There were stick people as well as many animals, some of the latter appearing to resemble goats. Troy suddenly remembered that his uncle had made particular mention of the goat-like designs, and he turned questioningly to his mentor.

"These goat figures. Do they have any significance?"

"Probably not, unless you are an old Aztec Indian," the old man stated from his reclined position on the cave's floor. "You must remember that it has been hundreds of years since my people journeyed to this place . . . I know not the true meaning of any of these figures—but I have heard that one called an 'ibex', which is the animal we now call goat. Perhaps your university books hold the answer, but I do know that it is a symbol of rock writing used only by the Aztec . . . The other—the bird-triangle, as you call it—is our sign for a duck. And, I don't know why they placed drawings of ducks in an area as dry as this. Perhaps at one time it was not so dry. Anyway, you wish to study the canyon more in the future. You will learn these things." He withdrew into thought, and Troy continued his survey and sketches of the walls.

There was a swishing sound as one of the horses brushed against a rock, and this announcement served to reacquaint both individuals with this stage upon which they played.

"The Paiute could have followed us in here," Troy said with a show of nervousness.

The Indian was interested, but not frightened. "I watched. No one followed us into the canyon. And, from the look of that trail we came down, no one but you and I know it exists—no one alive, that is . . . The Paiute, well they know the trail in from the north. And if they come, which I doubt, they will arrive by that path." Then the Indian was quiet and merely looked at Troy for some time. Finally he said, "We have rested long enough. Follow me . . . I must show you a certain place."

Troy followed as the Indian led the way downward along a narrow ledge to the canyon floor, his eyes dilating until the sun's brightness no longer forced him to blink.

The sandstone in this area was a pinkish hue, and here and there along the path was grotesquely shaped and undernourished conifers. Most vegetation was either scarce or nonexistent, and Troy marveled at how these trees must have struggled throughout the years against enormous odds, to spread roots that had searched every nook and crack in these rocks for precious drops of moisture.

Tecao suddenly halted near the center of a small grouping of pines. There he pointed to a pile of stones that had been placed in a pyramidal manner. He said simply, in a low tone, "Your Uncle Jim rests here."

Troy had to believe the Indian. Who else would have marked such a spot thusly, or why? . . . He recalled with a deep breath how his uncle had always been his childhood idol; about the many tales of adventure and intrigue, and how his own father would react with remorse upon learning of his brother's fate. For they had been much more than brothers. They had been friends and partners for years . . . Now this beloved uncle would forever occupy a tiny place in this forlorn canyon. Troy's hand went to the gold bracelet which dangled from the rawhide about his neck. Thoughts flashed to mind and he turned toward his friend who had wielded the instrument of death upon this cherished member of his family.

"You—you didn't—?"

The Indian read Troy's questioning eyes with the swiftness of lightning. "No," he interrupted. "He is very dead, but he is a whole man. Also, I tell you now that it was not I who killed his prospector friend of long ago, and placed his head among those of the Aztec warriors." He paused to lay a giant hand upon the younger man's shoulder, his eyes now as deep and as bronze as the canyon they stood in. "That was my cousin, Ithanan . . . Your uncle may have thought himself a good man, but most certainly he thought that I was not. And, as I've said, I knew neither of you at that time. Also, I had little choice in the matter." . . . His voice trailed off huskily.

Troy returned the other's intense stare. "I believe what you say, and also that he tried to kill you, as it would have been a natural thing for him to do . . . I cannot hold you responsible for his death, my friend."

The Indian seemed to blink almost imperceptibly as he withdrew several paces. "There is a thing I must do now. I must cross the canyon floor to the cave where the last of my people have lived. I shall see of their condition, if any remain. I fear it will not be a good visit. I ask that you return to our cave and not venture forth until my return. Be wary and watchful of every noise or movement, and make certain you do not go unarmed for even a short moment." He paused momentarily to squint upward at the sun, then said in an almost desultory manner, "I will return before the sun sets beyond the wall . . . And tomorrow—well, tomorrow you shall see your treasure, my young rider."

Troy took several long strides after the retreating Indian, with accompaniment of the older man upon his mind. But it was already too late. Only a flash of movement could be seen through the pinion grove, and the running footfalls were rapidly fading away. The young rider looked at his uncle's grave for a long moment, then he knelt and uttered aloud a brief but meaningful prayer. Thereafter he returned and began the long climb, lifting and re-holstering the .45 many times as he went.

CHAPTER 13

"**DYNAMITE!**" Virginia stared at the three, cylindrical explosives with instant fear and recognition, having seen such items in use by her father before. She looked briefly over the horse's rump from the rear of its saddle skirts and in the direction which Judd had taken on his quick scouting mission, then she wrapped the sticks once more and hurriedly stuffed the packet back into the saddle bag. She was buckling the strap when Hazelud clutched her arm from behind. Pulling violently, he spun her to the ground into an awkward, sitting position. Virginia remained motionless and thoroughly frightened upon the moment, her head reeling.

"Y'u had to see, didn't y'u? Yo'r cur'osity jest couldn't stand still!!! . . . Wal, now y'u know—"

"What—what are you going to do with that dynamite, Judd?" She breathed poignantly as she drew to a painful, standing position, half backing and stumbling away from him with a finger pointed accusingly in his general direction.

"Do?" Hazelud shot sharply as he poked at the saddle bag to make certain the dynamite was secure. Then he turned, taking a step toward her in disgust, with fingers knuckled on his hairy, ham-like hands. His eyes scorned her once more as he reiterated. "Do? I'll use it if I have ta! This stuff is my ace, if'n I have to play one."

Virginia's eyes suddenly blazed with the full realization of Judd's plan. "Judd Hazelud, you—you have no intention of letting Troy or Tecao, or—or anyone else, go unharmed. You don't intend to exchange their lives for the treasure, or—or me, either! You're going to kill both of them! . . . Oh, I wish I had a gun!"

Aroused as a wildcat, Virginia reached suddenly for a fist-sized rock at her feet. She would stop this man if she must kill him herself, and in any manner at her disposal! Raising the stone quickly, she paused to take point-blank aim at the advancing, menacing figure. But Judd Hazelud's feet suddenly froze to the sand, with his face whitening like flour as his eyes blinked and focused on something beyond her. Virginia stole a backward glance, then turned as she saw the Paiute.

The savage merely stood there, swarthy and unkempt; a picture of filth from head to toe as he grinned ruefully through long, scraggly hair. Around his feet were wrappings of hide, and a simple loincloth was his only other apparel than a thronged skin that held back the front portion of his dirty, lengthy hair. In his left hand he gripped a bow and several arrows, while cradled beneath his right arm was a rifle that appeared very similar to that of John Grayson's Winchester. Virginia started at this rifle and the entire scene, but kept her composure.

The Indian made no movement, but his eyes took in the young lady of the ranchero ravenously, and finally she shrank backward toward Judd, momentarily coming between him and the Paiute. Hazelud made a consideration about his six-gun, but that thought ended abruptly as the Indian uttered a low cry, summoning the remainder of his small band, which now rose to stand imposingly among the boulders to each side and beyond their leader.

THE SUN had long since edged beyond the canyon's brink. Troy paced the cave with worried, ceaseless steps, pausing for an occasional glance outward toward the darkened path that led to the canyon. No sound or shadow of the Indian broached the darkness. Then his attention was drawn by a scraping noise near the rear entrance, and he peered amid the shadows toward the ground-reined horses. Suddenly the dim outline of the animals was broken by a shadow that was moving slowly but steadily toward him. He watched stolidly for a moment . . . He hadn't expected Tecao to return by this route, but was exuberated when he realized that the Indian had returned, by any means. He stepped forward.

"Tecao! I thought you'd ne—"

The approaching figure emitted a blood-chilling scream as it launched itself upon the young rider, the noise renting the air as it echoed dramatically off the walls and sent the horses into a wheeling frenzy.

Troy's surprise was complete, and his recovery was not fast enough to avoid his assailant's first attack. He was thrust backward under the full weight of his adversary, and he felt the quickness and realism of pain as a sharp object parted the flesh on his shoulder. Gasping for air, his arms wind-milled upward, but his fists virtually slid from his opponent's greasy skin, and he was consumed by the unforgettable, acrid odor of the man. He tried forcing upward with both legs, but the weight of the enemy would not allow it, and a total feeling of helplessness all but overcame him as he saw the savage poise the weapon again, ready to plunge it downward.

Only a fraction of a second in length, the whistling sound sliced the darkness, ending a dull thud as though someone had punched the side of a drum. The Indian's body jerked forward, then his head snapped back as he propelled himself upward and over, his lifeless body flopping heavily across Troy's mid-section. Then strong arms were pulling Troy from under the would-be assassin, and he wretched as the pain shot from his shoulder through his body. His final recollection was that of reassurance—Tecao had returned.

Troy was awakened by shafts of sunlight that played along the eastern rim of the canyon. He looked about from his prone position near the mouth of the cavern, and the odor of fire and food filled his nostrils as he saw Tecao staring back at him over a small fire. The Indian had arranged dangle sticks containing strips of beef over the fire, and he arose to bring one of these morsels to Troy.

"You are a good sleeper for a wounded cub," Tecao stated good-naturedly, kneeling before his young companion. I trust you feel better now than last evening, my cub!"

Troy sat up with his free hand grasping his left shoulder. He felt the bandage a moment, then testily swung his left arm.

"Only a flesh cut," grunted the Indian in a reassuring tone, "but painful enough at that. How do you feel?" he repeated.

The events of the preceding evening spun through Troy's mind, and between gulps of the meat he answered as he queried hastily, "Who attacked me? . . . The Paiute did follow us into the canyon, eh?"

"No. Not Paiute—Ithanan," the old man stated impassively, as his gaze wandered from Troy out over the canyon. Then he sighed heavily. "He was Ithanan—my cousin, and the last of my people. Now he too is gone . . . They are all gone but Tecao." He exhaled again and paused long before continuing. "We are alone here, for the moment. And to this point in time the Paiute have believed the sculptured domes within our canyon to be evil creatures that have turned to stone, so they have feared to penetrate these walls. Ithanan and others before him have also been able to repel any attacks by those Paiute that haven't believed the story . . . Now—well, now I'm not so sure of what they may attempt."

Troy did not speak, but rather painfully gained his feet, watching as the Indian paced to the lip of the cave and stood for a moment . . . When Tecao turned, he seemed suddenly to be a much older man. Deep lines of worry were now etched into his face, and he looked as though all quickness and agility had suddenly deserted him. The old man looked squarely into the eyes of his young companion. His stance at the cliff's edge remained unchanged, but he said with the tone of one just returning from a deep well of thought, "It is time . . . Today I will show you the secret of my canyon, and, of my ancestor, Montezuma."

At mid-morning the seemingly-unlikely partners stood looking at the base of a vertical, sandstone cliff. Tecao pointed out several, scattered, bird-like petroglyphs and Troy himself located the tiny foot holes carved into the wall. Tecao, at Troy's request, allowed the two to be tied together by a strong length of rope—a climbing skill the youngster had long ago learned from his father. Then Troy slung a knapsack of tools over his shoulder. These preparations in order, the two slowly and painstakingly edged upward along the canyon wall, the safety rope hanging loosely between them.

Jim O'Neill's description of his hazardous climb had again been correct to a fault. The minute, gouged holes offered little support for either hand or toe, and certainly little area to pull or force against. Neither was the trace straight upward, but edged slowly to the right toward a shear cliff that appeared to rise from the lower part of the canyon to the very brink itself.

The climb seemed endless. Both men sweat profusely, their oily skin playing an even more dangerous part as they clung to the wall and its crevices with arms and knees as well as their hands and feet.

Troy could not resist several glances outward at the canyon, but he knew the first and foremost rule of climbing such a precipice, and thus not once did he cast his eyes straight downward. As they slowly progressed he found himself wondering at lengths about the skill and strength that would have been expended by the Aztecs who had carried treasure upward over the treacherous route. He also wondered as to the method he might employ to again lower such items as they may find. He vowed to ask Tecao about these thoughts as soon as the opportunity presented itself.

Suddenly he spied the huge spire directly over them. It had been invisible from either the cave or canyon floor, but there it was—an enormous wind and weather-carved sculpture of pink and red oxides. And, again true to his uncle's account, it did resemble a queen or stately figure wearing a dress. His heart beat wildly as the old Indian reached downward to aid his last, scrambling, upward thrust. Then they stood on a narrow ledge that wound about the statue's base.

The two leaned awkwardly on one another for a moment, bodies heaving to regain expended oxygen. When his breath had returned, Troy turned to survey the abyss. From this vantage point, five hundred feet above the canyon floor, the entire panoramic view spread out before them. The huge, tinted spires erupted from below and around them in truly majestic fashion. Troy had seen much red-rock during his young lifetime, but nothing that compared to this breathtaking sight—a scene that had been preparing for this moment for millions of years. The Indian interrupted with a pointing finger.

SUDDENLY THE ARCHWAY HE
HAD LONG INVISIONED
STARED BACK AT HIM.

134

"See . . . over there." His extended hand was aimed directly across the canyon to the opposite wall, where Troy shifted his gaze to discover several caves, dug deeply in and slightly above the canyon floor. "There," Tecao repeated. "That is where I lived as a small boy. It was our home, as it belonged to many before my family . . . As you can see, its position was chosen wisely."

Troy had to nod in agreement. The location of the caves had indeed afforded their occupants excellent vision of the entire canyon, and moreover an exceptional view of the point at which they now stood. He dwelt upon the thought that it was an exciting event to look forward to—to one day have an opportunity to explore those caves.

Tecao turned along the path and ended the youngster's thoughts. "Come. This way."

They rounded the base of the spire and emerged into the open. The spot was as flat as an iron and about the size of a large corral. It had been carved into the wall of the precipice as if by a knife, and one could see at a glance that such a shelf could only have been carved by human methods. He marveled at this for but a moment, then peered ahead toward the solid, vertical wall. The head-high archway that he had long envisioned stared back at him. Just as also described, it was obviously a sealed doorway, constructed of various size and colored stones, with the spaces between chinked with a dark hardened and matted, clay-like substance. There also, in rough, triangular fashion were the seventeen niches in which lay the powdering remains of human bone and teeth. And, on the rock below yet another shelf, where it had no doubt fallen with the aid of some scavenger, lay a skull that was nearly intact—undoubtedly that of the prospector, Grace.

Tecao said nothing. Rather he proceeded carefully and somewhat reverently to remove the human remains and place them aside in a small pile.

Troy watched the old man work for a time, wondering what thoughts might be going through the Indian's mind at this moment, then he removed a small pick from his sack and began to hack at the hardened clay that cemented the rocks. He worked carefully, beginning with a few small stones near the very center of the arch, and was surprised at the ease with which they shifted and came apart. The small boulders had been carefully sized and interlocked, and were several in depth, forming a barrier about two feet in thickness.

"I've broken through!" the youngster exclaimed.

The old Indian moved quickly to lean above Troy and look through the tiny opening to the blackness beyond. Suddenly he stepped swiftly backward, pulling the young rider with him. His eyes were transfixed upon the opening, and a puzzled, worried look was frozen upon his face.

139

CHAPTER 14

TROY SPUN ABOUT, releasing himself from the Indian's grasp. "What' wrong? What did you see?"

Tecao gazed long and enigmatically at the black hole, saying nothing. Finally a look of revelation flashed upon his face.

"I remember now! The huge stone at the top! We must do this just right, as that opening is designed to collapse upon us. It was built just that way, and it will stop all but the most careful entry into the vault . . . My father told me of this many years ago. I am sorry I did not remember sooner, my young friend."

"Now, we must proceed with caution, working from the exact center and from the bottom upward, leaving all the stones to each side. If we break the arch we will release a long, large block of stone—one that must remain supported by that archway. That stone is not only large enough to block the cave entrance for all time, but it is large enough to bury you and me beneath it as well!"

Thus the work continued, and in short order the men had created an opening at the very bottom that was large enough to enable them to crawl through. Troy then removed a small torch from his sack, lit it, and handed it ceremoniously to the Indian. "After you," he stated with a salacious grin.

The Indian made no reply as he knelt to crawl through the opening, thrusting the torch through first. As soon as the Indian disappeared through the rocks, Troy followed, pulling the knapsack behind.

They emerged into a large chamber. Both men regained their feet and looked about as the flickering torch cast a wavering, eerie light around them.

The walls were vertical and appeared smooth but for a variety of petroglyphs, while the ceiling ran at an elevation far over their heads and was like-wise flat in appearance. Then the young rider's slowly dilating eyes began to focus toward the rear wall, where uneven objects cast back the flickering torchlight as though it were being reflected from a thousand, individual mirrors.

They advanced cautiously, the scuffling of their feet and even their breathing echoing back from all angles of the chamber. Then they were standing directly before the objects, which were positioned singularly in some places and at others stacked so high as to tower near the ceiling. They looked on, wide-eyed with amazement.

The larger items were silver and gold vases, nearly a dozen in all, their sides finely etched with designs and encrusted with sparkling jewels. These vases were placed in a manner of prominence upon solid gold and silver discs, some as large as cartwheels. A few shorter yet larger-diameter vases had been placed directly upon the floor, and from within these glared enormous pearls and precious gems, including emeralds the size of a man's fist. These seemed like huge, staring eyeballs. Placed at random in wall niches were solid gold castings in the shape of dogs, jaguars, ducks, alligators and monkeys, along with several silver and gold plaques. Many of these plaques were also encrusted with gems. A large stack of jewel-inlaid body armor had been carefully placed in one corner—perhaps the very armor belonging to the Aztec warriors that had performed this burial.

"By all the Saints and all that's Holy!" Troy breathed forth, the very shock of it overcoming him, "I don't believe this! . . . I just don't believe it's real!" He reached to steady himself against the Indian's shoulder.

Tecao extended a helping hand. "I told you, my young rider. It is here—more treasure than but a chosen few have ever seen. Perhaps all the kings within your history books, when combined, have never seen such a gathering of wealth."

There was no noise in the chamber as the Indian kept a pensive moment, then he said hesitantly, "And I—I have now broken a trusted secret of my ancestry. Broken it, and their trust, by bringing you here and opening this chamber to you . . . I will not be—"

"No!" Troy broke in passionately. "You have broken no existing law. It is an old law that has been outdated with the passing of time and the circumstances of time. You are the last of your people, and the secret would have died with you!"

"Perhaps—"

"It is the fact! . . . Besides, I had the map and my uncle's account. I would have found the treasure in due time . . . That is, if I had survived the Paiute, Ithanan's attack, this climb—and the possible collapse of this chamber, among other things." The young rider from Arizona was pensive, then spoke out respectfully, "Tecao, my friend, it seems I owe you my very life many times over, but it is best this way, and by bringing me here you have not betrayed your people."

The old Indian moved his lips as though chewing these facts over, then spoke out, "To make what you say the truth, young rider, what you indeed owe me is not your life at such a moment, but your future hereafter . . . You have made your promise to this old man. You must use this wealth to build your university, and to further peace and understanding among our peoples. If you do this, then I will know that I have done no wrong."

Troy glanced rapidly around the room, his eyes coming to rest upon the Indian. "The archaeological value within these walls is priceless itself, and there is perhaps enough wealth here to build a hundred such universities. I could not spend the money that is here in my lifetime, and I confess that I really have no idea just what such a treasure is worth—many millions of dollars, I suppose . . . But, I will keep my promise to you, remain assured of that. I will build the university I spoke of and do all that is within my power to further the respect and understanding among our races."

Tecao seemed momentarily placated, and Troy paced astatically about the cave once again, unable to convince himself that it all was real. He touched and handled the items at will. The Indian looked on in silence as the strong youngster struggled mightily and was barely able to move some of the heavier discs and vases.

Finally Troy hesitated to turn an uplifted, questioning eyebrow toward Tecao. "Two of us would never be able to navigate that cliff with some of the treasure, let alone get them out of the canyon safely."

The old man stood thoughtfully, the flickering torchlight playing eerily upon his facial lines. Then he rejoined, "You've made a wise observation. It is a fact that it took the warriors nearly a year to get the treasure in its place. But, my friend, they did not carry it up from the canyon floor as you have in mind—it was lowered from the cliff's edge, above. They worked in pairs, using long ropes, somewhat like a human chain . . . But, as you can also observe, we now have the same situation in reverse. A long drop into the sand below will do little if any damage at all to most of the things . . . The vases are an exception, of course. But I have a good idea."

"It's your decision," replied Troy.

"Well, you have said that there is much wealth here. If that is so, let us take but a small portion of it now—a few items we can carry down the face of the cliff and a few others that can be dropped safely to the canyon floor. That amount we can easily pack out of the canyon with the horses, and the rest you can return for one day . . . It has, after all, been in this place some three hundred years. We will patch the entrance, and it is not likely to fly out of its nest and away before your return."

The young rider beamed at his companion. "You're correct, partner. And, we'd better get about it—that torch isn't going to last much longer!" He knelt to proceed the Indian through the opening, pausing only long enough to cast an upward glance at the massive, square-hewn stone over the entrance. The death missile was clearly as large as Tecao's lean-to!

The first order of business was to enlarge the cave opening by a small measure. Once done, they then struggled at lengths to wrestle and roll several of the large, gold and silver discs from the chamber to the cliff's edge. Troy considered the jeweled body armor to be the utmost in historical value, thus they placed a considerable amount of it outside the cave. Then Troy placed several of the smaller artifacts and a few of the larger emeralds and gems within his knapsack. At this point it seemed useless to haul more items from the chamber, as he considered those already outside to be priceless as well as all that they and the pack animals could remove from the canyon in one trip. He would take the Indian's advice and return to the treasure another time, perhaps as soon as he could form an expedition to do so. He mused upon that moment of realization . . . An expedition of his own! This would be a reality, for barring any unseen misfortune, he was now not only a rich man but would acquire immediate fame through all the archaeological circles around the world. Forming a real expedition would not be difficult, rather the problem would fall in the choosing of those to accompany him. That could indeed become a challenge. And, there would be the danger wrought by other treasure seekers once the word was spread . . . At this point he made mental note to put confidence of its exact location and its circumstance in absolutely no one else until certain of that person's complete trust and reliability.

"I know not where your mind is wandering, young rider." The Indian thus interrupted the dreamer with a knowing smile. "But we've got to get this job done. Now, go back down the trace carefully. While you are about it, I will drop these treasures one by one over the edge. When you are safely below you move them aside—those you can handle alone. I will then follow, and we will wrestle them onto the pack horses and be on our way. Hurry now. The hours escape quickly."

Troy glanced at the sun that was beginning to nudge the canyon wall overhead. Then he looked at the Indian, a smirking expression overcoming his face. "I shall arrest my silliness long enough to do as you say." He hesitated, turning just before rounding the base of the spire. "I—well, I was just thinking."

"What?" grunted the Indian.

"Well, believe it or not, I was just wondering when you and I might go together to fish—down where your big fish run. Rather a stupid thought, I suppose, for what's happening right now."

The old Indian's face erupted with an impish grin, and Troy turned toward the trail downward.

The climb upward proved not as difficult as the descent. Troy must look downward this time to assure proper footing, and his head spun constantly with a dizziness caused by the height. Also, this time there was no insurance rope fastened between friends. The knapsack grew increasingly heavy with the weight of its treasure, and try as he did to maintain it in a comfortable position, it continually swung from side to side, keeping him unsteady and off balance. Troy finally decided that its contents would be of little value to a dead man, and thus removed it at a position affording him sure footing. Then he flung it far out and upward toward the canyon trail, watching and then listening as it arched and dropped with an audible thud near the boulders where the steps began. Thus unencumbered by that burden, he turned to the downward trek.

A faint sound, somewhat resembling a muffled shout, suddenly echoed around him amid the sandstone. Then it was repeated, and grew louder. Troy froze against the wall, his eyes flicking about the portion of the canyon that was visible to him. He saw no movement, but a second sound now floated to him and echoed once more—this time it was an unmistakable scream, and it came from above! He searched upward, but the wall's angle blocked from view even the ledge upon which the Indian had stood. Filled with a terror from he knew not what, he quickly renewed the downward journey, near the bottom gaining a position that would afford him a view of the canyon's rim.

Upon the brink and precariously close to the edge were tiny, ant-like figures. Several of these remained quite rigid, while others seemed to move about within a small area. All were unrecognizable from the distance, and then there came a sudden flask of fire-red hair! Troy became unnerved. Virginia! No, she couldn't possibly be here at this canyon! . . . But suddenly that flash of hair told him she was here—no one with hair as easy to recognize as hers would be within a hundred miles of this spot. His breath shortened and his heart now pumped like a steam engine as he looked upward, blinking against the sun's rays.

Now another movement captured his eyes. This too seemed impossible. There it was, however: a human, fly-like creature, rapidly scaling the shear wall above the treasure cave. Tecao! The youngster watched with a feeling of total helplessness as the old Indian continued to climb without an instant of hesitation.

Had there been another trace carved into the face of that cliff? If so, Troy had not spotted it from the shelf above. Yet, it could be so—Tecao had said that the treasure had been lowered from the canyon's edge, and that could mean a trail of some sort, if ever so minute and hazardous! In any event, the Indian was now in the process of performing a most miraculous feat, and the speed of his climb seemed to increase as he moved upward . . .

Suddenly there came the dull report of gunfire from above, and Troy watched as one of the figures at the brink pitched crazily forward into the void. Troy looked on in a petrified state as Tecao gained the rim, paused momentarily, then disappeared above it with a mighty leap. The tempo of gunshots and their echoes grew to a crescendo. Then there was a silence and lack of movement upon the cliff, and a continuation of movement as two figures appeared, seemingly to grapple with one another at a point dangerously near the edge. Troy now discerned the bronze figure of Tecao, but the other was uncertain. Then the entwined combatants lurched over the brink, still locked in mortal combat.

There came an ear-splitting and deafening eruption from above that shook the cliff upon which Troy narrowly clung. Then the youngster was hurled backward from his foothold . . . While falling, he was momentarily but acutely aware of a rumbling not unlike that of an active volcano. Then all went black around and within his body.

CHAPTER 15

JOHN GRAYSON reined up the posse with scarcely a quarter mile remaining between his riders and the canyon. The horses seemed more grateful than ever for the brief halt, having been under constant pressure from rider and spur these two days running.

Grayson, reasonably familiar with the terrain, was likewise reasonably certain that their quarry would be close beyond this barren wash which now separated them from a strip of land along the canyon's edge. There would also be little cover between this protective wash and the canyon, so whatever move was in order must be done with expediency and total surprise. These facts in mind, he quickly pondered the situation.

John and Martha Grayson had first been overcome with grief when Virginia did not return from her afternoon ride. However, it had required mere moments upon the following morning to discover her plight—when a rapid dispersion of Grayson's riders, who had already spent the sleepless night searching for signs by lantern light, had shown the scuffle and trail of horses that led to the north from Tecao's lean-to.

Thus Grayson and six of his best riders had set upon the northward trail, traveling as rapidly as the terrain allowed and becoming increasingly alarmed at the signs along the way. The dearth of rainfall throughout the area had left a trail to be followed at a gallop, and they made use of the advantage.

A rather worried inspection ensued at the position where Troy and the Indian had undergone siege, they having found it clearly marked by circling buzzards. But their findings include the remains of two Paiute warriors along with numerous, spent .45 cartridges.

Grayson's men had needed little coaxing to ply onward through the night, and thus arrived after their second sleepless night at a scene where much harried action had obviously occurred. Here, joining the boot prints of Virginia and her heavy male captor, were the mingling of light Indian tracks. One of the riders also picked up a short length of saddle strap, which another hand quickly pointed out was that belonging to Judd Hazelud.

Upon having his suspicion fully confirmed by this find, Grayson bellowed, "By the Lord! I'll kill Judd or anyone else if they've harmed so much as one of Ginny's red hairs! Six of 'em or a thousand—makes no difference to me!" He swung to the saddle and led the way at a speed almost resembling a charge.

*   *   *

A PAIUTE SCOUT rejoined the band, immediately confronting its leader with a flurry of comments and signs. All of his remarks and gestures were unintelligible to either of their captives. These individuals, trail worn and frightened but otherwise unharmed by the Paiute renegades, sat their horses and looked over these proceedings intently.

Judd Hazelud turned to the unkempt young woman at his side and whispered, "I git nothin' from this heah talk, but thet Ingin' scout 'peers to argue with the boss one. Ce'tainly it 'peers he's a tellin' aboot two men up ahead somewheres. An' iff'n I savvy his arm wavin', why he's sayin' thet they're down in thet canyon doin' something . . . Thet boss man, 'peers he wants no part of thet canyon!"

Virginia looked at Judd briefly then continued her surveillance of the Indians, remaining non-committal toward her former captor. Gradually, the realization had come upon her that for the first time in this hazardous venture she and this man were somewhat allies. Strange partners they were indeed, but nonetheless now placed in a circumstance whereby their lives may very well depend upon one another. And, she found herself wondering, would Judd Hazelud think only of himself just now, or might he assist her as well in any escape attempt?

Presently Virginia spoke out, more in thinking aloud than to the cowboy. "Certainly the Paiute have been aware of the treasure legend for many years. But father has told me that for some strange reason they will not enter the canyon to look for it. They've roamed this area for several hundred years, killing whites and some of Tecao's people as well . . . I'm afraid that they will not hesitate to bring instant death to us as well as to Tecao and—and Troy." Her voice faded, then came alive again as her eyes flashed at Hazelud. "We must make an escape—or at least an attempt. We can't just—just—"

The argument among the savages had come to an abrupt conclusion, and hard hands grasped the reins of Virginia's mustang, pulling her several yards distant of Hazelud. Then the Indians mounted their bareback pintos, with several moving into the slot between the captives. Thus they were led forward at a walk, advancing toward the canyon's brink in a slow-moving wall.

Judd Hazelud suddenly jerked at the reins and vaulted sideways onto the Indian nearest him. Other Indians rapidly closed in, but Judd had enveloped the man's neck with a giant arm. There was a loud crack and the Indian's neck was broken, rending death an instant before the two rolled into the dirt. But this moment of diversion ended swiftly as one of the band moved into position where he swung his rifle downward and knocked Hazelud to a senseless position beside the dead savage. Judd was pulled to his feet, where he stood dazed for but a moment before being prodded onward in animal-fashion, finally to stand wavering upon the very edge of the shear cliff.

Virginia's thoughts turned now to certain death, and her only recourse seemed to be the animal upon which she rode. She started to spur her mount to action. This too was instantly thwarted, as scaly hands unceremoniously hauled her from the saddle. Now she was forced forward alongside Judd, and was halted in a position directly behind the Indian leader, who now looked downward and pointed excitedly toward something below. Then other Indians moved cautiously forward, and they too looked over the edge, some with mixed signs of apprehension, others assuming evil grins and making jesting remarks.

Virginia strained forward slightly, but her vantage point included only the ghastly width and depth of the canyon. She struggled to move backward, but horny fingers dug into her shoulders from the rear, holding her helplessly in position. What was now to be her certain fate would serve to bring Troy and Tecao out of the canyon—for it must be they that these Indians had spotted below—and they too would be slaughtered.

The Paiute leader began to laugh. It was low and guttural at first, then he tilted back and laughed tauntingly, almost with a loud gloat, each time culminating with a boisterous whooping sound. He was gaining in courage and it was also evident that he had attracted someone's attention from below, for now he preceded each display by jostling both captives from side to side, then pausing to point and whoop again and again. Virginia and Judd stood wholly frightened for their lives now, as death must be eminent.

Close range, pin-point gunfire suddenly erupted from the sides and to the rear. Virginia was hurriedly released, her own weight sending her backward from the cliff's edge to a sitting position. Her captor had been gunned down, and then the Indian that held Judd lurched aside to pitch crazily over the edge. Horses and Indians swirled together in a dust cloud, with one Indian after another spurting blood at the triggers of Grayson's men.

The surprise attack was over in an instant, with Indian ponies running free and headlong from the spot, and John Grayson and his riders piling off their mounts to assume command.

The smell of burned powder was drifting off with the echoes of gunfire as Virginia's voice suddenly floated above the melee. "No! Help me!" She fainted away as the Paiute leader grasp her in front of him, with his back to the cliff and eyes bulging red as fire.

Grayson threw up a hand as several riders made signs toward raising their weapons again. "Do nothing! He's crazy an' he'll throw her over!" The order was loud and strong as he carefully approached the two. The Indian held the obvious advantage and it was clear he would risk is own life along with that of Virginia.

Suddenly all but the Indian and his captive stood in petrified awe, as a hand and arm appeared out of the canyon's depths behind the Indian. In that hand glinted a long knife, which quickly whistled through the air to lodge into the savage's back. The mortally wounded Paiute flopped aside, then kicked over upon his back. The knife was driven through, its point now exposed amid the spouting blood from the Indian's chest.

The girl from the ranchero fell forward into her father's outstretched hands. It grew quiet, and Grayson looked beyond his awakening and unharmed daughter toward this bronze hero of the fight. Tecao stood tall, but his aging body heaved mightily from the strain of the climb. A semblance of a smile came upon his gasping lips, and he looked about the gathering in a somewhat detached manner.

"How in the world—well, how did you—" Grayson sputtered, unable to complete the question.

"There is an old trace up the canyon wall," Tecao replied with recognition of the other's thoughts. "At the moment I'm not sure just how."

Grayson's thoughts quickened. "Where is Troy?"

"The young rider is safe in the canyon below us. He is alone, but I will return for him." The Indian then hastened to ask, "How did Virginia come to be here?"

"Hazelud. He took Ginny captive and forced her to accompany him. My guess would be that he intended to kill the both of y'u—an' perhaps Virginia as well . . . What he was really after was thet treasure, ta keep fer himself."

Tecao's eyes quickly flicked around the gathering. "That treasure, if any exists, is also safe in the canyon below . . . . Now! I have a duty to do before this is over . . . Where is Hazelud?"

It was obvious that the outlaw had been forgotten amid the preceding chaos by his captors and the posse alike. Now all eyes swept the area.

This was the outlaw's cue and he was on schedule. Hazelud edged from behind a pack horse and moved slowly along near the rim, making certain all could see him clearly. In one hand he brandished a dynamite stick, and in the other, a match. As he moved, his eyes flicked from Tecao to Grayson and back again in a constant rhythm. He was mad, and every inch of him showed the fact.

"This here's my ace, Grayson, an' I'm playin' it right here an' now! . . . I want y'u all ta git on them hosses an' ride out, an' I want it done right now!" The talker then leaned toward the canyon with a scornful look, moving as if to prepare to strike the match against his leg. "If'n y'u don't do it right now, I'll jest drop this over the side an' blow thet young lover o' hern clear to hail!"

Animals and men alike faded backward in a sudden wave, and Grayson half dragged his daughter along in the frightening, yet decisive, moment. Virginia grabbed at her father and dug her boots into the ground despairingly.

"No, father! We must stop Judd! He—he means to kill Troy anyway! He doesn't care about himself now, and he'll kill all of us if he can!"

Grayson suddenly knew that his daughter spoke the absolute truth. Now there was a moment of indecision, and it was in this split second that Tecao made a standing leap toward Hazelud.

Tecao's leap fell short and he landed in an awkward, crouched position near the outlaw. He sprung again, and this time grasped Hazelud by a leg that had been swung to meet him. Judd spun from the Indian's grasp. Suddenly he held the dynamite outward toward his adversary as one might brandish a sword. He had lit the fuse!

Virginia screamed in terror, "He will kill us all! Oh, someone—someone stop him!"

Grayson's six-gun flew from its holster and other hands followed suit, but the Indian made a last, desperate lunge which allowed him to grab the wild-eyed Hazelud. They were wrestling in an upright position, and somehow the Indian managed to hold the strong cowboy's arm in a fixed, upward arc. But Tecao's remaining strength would not allow him to wrench the dynamite away. The helpless onlookers pushed backward once more as they saw the fuse burning dangerously close. Then, with a last, almost super-human effort, the aging Indian wheeled and forced Judd with him to the very edge of the precipice. Then Judd's eyes took on a mortally-frightened glaze, as the two, locked together by Tecao's arms, pitched into space.

A moment later the air was devastated by a roaring explosion. The watchers were forced backward abruptly by the concussion of the exploding dynamite, and the ground literally sank away at their feet. The huge, jutting mass before them—thousands of tons of earth and rock—had been released to plummet unchecked into the canyon below.

CHAPTER 16

VIRGINIA lingered long and dangerously close to the fatal precipice, and under acute protest from John Grayson, who had finally but unwillingly ordered that a temporary camp be set up a safe distance from the rim.

The young lady of the Ranchero Johnson looked on morbidly and with little interest as the ranch hands removed and buried the several Paiute bodies, returning her gaze often toward the canyon's bottomless depths. In turn she talked and prayed aloud and to herself . . . Why had God taken her lover away? Why had He not spared him, for he must be gone . . . No! He could yet be alive, for somehow he might have escaped the landslide . . . No. It was obvious to all that the floor of the canyon below had been decimated or bombarded unmercifully by tons of earth and hurtling stone. Hadn't her father repeatedly and emphatically told her that there had been no possible way for her young rider to escape? And, hadn't Tecao himself said that the rider was below them on the canyon floor? That part of the canyon had been totally and permanently damaged, and alas, there could be no hope. Her young lover was gone, and with him had vanished their hopes and dreams—dreams of a future together; of Troy's becoming an archaeologist and of his want to one day begin a university of his own—one that would be dedicated to a better understanding among the whites and Indians . . . Indians . . . Tecao! He would return no more to watch the sunset from his lean-to by the canyon wall . . . Perhaps he was the very last of his people . . .

"Father, I—I am ready to go home now." Virginia approached him at first light on the second morning, her chin high but with telltale circles beneath her eyes that spoke of a sleepless night.

John Grayson gave his daughter a wise and knowing look as he buttoned his jacket against the coolness of coming autumn.

* * *

THE FIRST SENSATION was a buzzing within his head, this to be followed by a feeling of weightlessness and a lacking of all senses but the taste and smell of stale air. Gradually his ability to feel returned, and then the young rider discovered that he could move nothing but his right arm. He lay flat upon his back, pinned by an immense weight of rock and earth. Finally he recognized that he was in a crevice between two huge boulders and that a small pocket had formed around him. He was somehow able to see! He peered outward into the darkness, and through a narrow slit several stars blinked back in the distance that was night.

His legs still remained solidly pinned, and he pondered a way to free them without releasing another slide from above. Then he carefully picked away at these rocks, edging each out of the widening hole to freedom. Suddenly he was able to sit upright, and from this position was able to work until both legs were free. He tested them warily, drawing each forward by bending the knee. Neither appeared broken, but the right one throbbed painfully with each movement, and matted blood showing through the trousers showed signs of cuts or other superficial wounds.

Now Troy O'Neill crawled painstakingly outward, widening the entrance to his would-be burial vault as he proceeded . . . Then he was suddenly outside, and free!

The young rider from Arizona stood clear and painfully tested each leg once more as he surveyed the black wall above. The cascade of earth had rendered it totally unrecognizable.

The events of the day began to flash through his mind's eye . . . Had it even occurred today? How long he had remained buried was uncertain. Suddenly he looked up, speaking to the stars and the moon that shone through the night. "Thank God!" he cried aloud, "I'm alive! . . . But I have lost my dearest friend, for Tecao, with his many miracles, could not have survived such a fall, or that landslide . . . And the treasure is gone as well—the treasure that would have allowed me to keep my solemn promise to him. Gone with the cliff . . . The cliff! Virginia!" She too had been upon that cliff! He halted, grief stricken, then cried aloud once more, "God, you have taken two of the dearest people on this earth! I will never forgive you for this!" His pathetic voice merely echoed amid the jumble of sandstone around him, and his eyes returned again to this landscape. It was bleak and now seemed without meaning. Finally he began to hobble toward the trail that would lead him to the cave. "Sundown," he proclaimed aloud once more. "I must get up to Sundown . . . With his help I can make—"

He halted as his eyes fell upon a huge, glittering object that lay squarely in his path. He fell quickly and grasped it. One of the emeralds! Then he groped about on his knees, examining the moonlit area. His hand touched something made of cloth, and suddenly he had the knapsack in his clutches. Hurriedly he opened it and peered in at the jewels and artifacts. Then, tearfully he looked upward toward the heavens he had cursed but moments before. "Thank you, God! At least you have given me the means to make part of the dream come true!" Then he regained his feet, and placing the sack over his shoulder struck forward along the upward trail. He knew now that he would make it out, and what he must do.

Sundown tossed his head and snorted an almost scolding welcome as the young rider sank to the stream pocket to drink his fill. This accomplished, Troy secured the sack and a canteen of fresh water to the horse's bridle. Leaving the heavy saddle behind, he grabbed at the animal's reins. Sundown, seeming to grasp both the urgency and danger of the situation, needed no further coaxing as Troy knotted the reins about his right arm and headed the animal upward and into the dangerous dark trace.

Troy was neither physically nor mentally aware of the treacherous climb from the canyon. Rather, he was totally dependent upon the horse. They stumbled together, slid together, and often rested together, with the young cowboy virtually dragged and bounced along in the animal's dusty wake.

Sundown was a powerful animal, but the climb under these conditions was nearly an impossibility. He lathered profusely and finally wheezed a bloody foam which trickled backward and ran in rivulets along his neck and legs, eventually to become matted with dirt in his fetlocks.

Daylight was breaking over the eastern wall of the canyon as horse and man stumbled the remaining yards upward and over the final break. Once above the obstacle, Sundown sank first to his knees and then lay over on his side, heaving mightily. Troy collapsed into a heap at the horse's side, his arm still tied to the reins.

It had not been long, as the sun remained low in the eastern sky when the noise penetrated his ears. It was the unmistakable rumble of many hoof beats, and mingled with this was the cry of voices—riders! It stemmed from the wash just beyond, and he rose painfully to his feet, shouting in the direction of the pounding hoof beats. He could not see them, but it became rapidly clear that the riders did not let up speed. Finally, he turned his attention to the horse, gesturing with his tied arm. "Come on, Sundown! We're almost—." The beautiful sorrel made no movement, and the youngster hobbled to where he could pass his hand over the animal's head. Then slowly he untied the knotted reins from his arm . . . Another loved one had given a life for the rider from Arizona.

THE YOUNG LADY at the ranchero hung to the rear of the pack as it moved out and down the wash paralleling the canyon. Her heart was heavy with a longing to wait here—for a hope that she knew would not be coming. Then those ahead passed from view over the last fault, leaving her and the canyon behind and alone with one another. She reined up her mount and cast a last, hopeless and longing look toward the gigantic amphitheater and its ragged escarpments . . . She would retain this moment and this place always within her heart—and she would return to it again and again.

Virginia's wet eyes flicked across the rim rock and then returned to focus upon one small spot. Something had appeared to move! No! . . . Yes! He heart nearly exploded within as her eyes unbelievingly devoured a slowly moving, faltering, staggering figure. It now moved toward her, one almost death-defying step after another. Then an arm waved falteringly through the air to drop heavily and throw its bearer out of balance and downward into the sand . . .

"Troy! Oh, my God! Thank the good God! It is you!" Her cries of joy seemed so loud as to echo forever off the ragged landscape. Then she spurred her mount and rode at a full gallop, to dismount and fling herself to the ground beside her fallen love.

EPILOGUE

THE YEAR WAS 1900, and the Arizona Territory would not gain statehood for an additional twelve years. However, a university in Arizona had been granted a charter in the autumn of the eighteen hundreds, and began instructions in 1891.

Among the university's sixth graduating class sat a tall, lean young man of twenty-four. His keen, green eyes sparkled outward from under an auburn mop of hair and he seemed to radiate all that was strength, excitement and adventure.

Jim O'Neill searched among the onlookers as he sat waiting his turn to walk the short steps and receive his diploma.

They were there: his father, Professor of Archaeology and President of the university he had created—graying somewhat, but with a look that was clear and proud; his mother, dabbing at her pretty cheeks and green eyes with a tear-stained handkerchief; and Bell, his lively young sister, now a freshman at the same university and the self-proclaimed watchdog of the family ranch up in Utah.

"James Troy O'Neill," the speaker's voice rang above the crowd, "A degree in Religion, with minor degrees in both the

Science of Archaeology and Indian Education . . . A first at this university, and first in his class."

Jim O'Neill had no ears for the drumming noise of his classmate's cheers as he took long strides toward the podium. He was deep in his own thoughts.

Jim knew the significance of the diploma he was about to receive. It was to mark the beginning of a long and adventuresome religious and humanitarian quest. He was devout in his religion, and obsessed with the idea of carrying it to the lives of others. But it was destined that his first quest would take him within a distant canyon—a canyon filled with gigantic sandstone spires and domes; where huge, red pinnacles rise as chessmen might from a giant chessboard . . . A canyon that had yet to bear complete testimony to its ancestry, and also one where a tall, bronze, legendary figure was sometimes said to be seen moving in ghostly fashion along its many, unconquerable traces.

THE END